Also by John D. Husband

Single Over Thirty
witty insights into the single life
(now that you're not a kid anymore)

Si jeunesse savait, si vieillesse pouvait.
(If youth but knew and age but could.)
-- Henri Estienne, 1594

MAGGIE AGAIN

MAGGIE AGAIN

a novel

JOHN D. HUSBAND

Talywain Press

Publisher's Cataloging-in-Publication

(Provided by Quality Books, Inc.)

Husband, John D.

Maggie Again : a novel / by John D. Husband.

p. cm.

LCCN 2007900433

ISBN-13: 978-0-9741942-6-4

ISBN-10: 0-9741942-6-3

1. Teenagers--Indiana--Fiction. 2. Time travel--
Fiction. 3. Indiana--Fiction. 4. New York (N.Y.)--
Fiction. 5. Science fiction. I. Title.

PS3608.U83M34 2007   813'.6

QBI07-600038

Dedication

This book is dedicated to my brothers, Tom, Phil, Bert and Alan who, with me, spent all their childhood summers on Grandpa's farm in the company of our 11 Davenport, Dungan and Trumbower cousins.

MAGGIE
AGAIN

Chapter One

The village of Cobblers Eddy, Indiana is just a collection of houses, shops and barns strung along a two lane concrete road and surrounded by rolling farmland that extends to the horizon in all directions. The west edge of town is defined by the West Fork of the White River about sixty miles before it meets the East Fork and flows lazily down the Illinois-Indiana border to join the Wabash. The few dozen residents of Cobblers Eddy are less precise about the village's other boundaries.

They are equally vague about the swirl of water in the river for which the town was named. Most have never seen it by reason of indifference, or because it isn't always visible. The eddy is caused by an underwater rock ledge that juts out into the river and can only be seen if the water level is just right. When swift currents hit the ledge, they flow abruptly back upstream for 50 feet or so, until they lose their momentum. That backward flowing water causes an eddy as it speeds past the downstream water — much as two rapidly moving weather systems spawn tornadoes when they swipe past each other. Provided the river is neither too shallow nor too deep, the splashing, ageless eddy is clearly visible. And anyone who cares enough to look can get a clear view of the bobbing leaves and sticks that accumulate in its vortex much as its namesake village has over time collected houses and shops — never growing noticeably larger or smaller and seeming not to change essentially with the passing years.

Whereas the river eddy may be rare, there are a thousand villages like Cobblers Eddy, maybe more, sprinkled across the North American continent — clusters of old sheds, weathered barns and neat clapboard houses that sprout along rural highways like tufts of grass in the cracks between city sidewalks. Most of these little villages were seeded some time in the 19th century by a remote rural crossroads that attracted a church or a feed store or a blacksmith shop and a house or two. Then perhaps a general store joined that small nucleus and maybe a barber shop, a few sheds, a barn and a machine shop to fix broken plows, John Deere tractors, and other farm machinery.

Without a major industry to attract new people, villages like Cobblers Eddy seldom grow large enough to support their own local governments. Instead they depend upon the county for road maintenance and emergency services. Once established, these little villages seem to freeze in time, neither growing nor diminishing. Successive generations move into and out of their ageless houses, work the distant fields, and milk the cows as the years tumble into decades and beyond.

Today, passing motorists see Cobblers Eddy as a sort of pastoral stereopticon, a three dimensional picture of old time America, its quaint values preserved uncorrupted by technology, rock music, fast food, and beer in cans. The motorists see white clapboard houses, rustic barns, and amber fields of grain sweeping in lazy rhythm to the wind, and they dream of simpler days. They catch a glimpse of clothes strung on a line in the back yard and of barefoot children with dirty faces frolicking about unattended and think they have had a privileged peek into the past.

They smile wistfully, perhaps, and drive on by.

It's a timeless place, this Cobblers Eddy, isolated, self sufficient, unchanged, and unchanging.

Chapter Two

"Death doesn't scare me," someone had once told Margaret Stone, "it's those last few moments of life that I'm terrified of." After 25 years as office manager for The American Equity Insurance Group on New York's East 44th Street, Margaret felt the same way about retirement.

She wanted today to be over. Tomorrow had to be better. No matter that the paychecks would stop and she'd miss her friends and the routine. Anything had to be better than the agony and celebrity of being a departing faithful servant to the company.

Seated behind her desk in a cluttered 35th floor office, she swiveled toward the window and the splendor of the New York City skyline stretched grandly before her. She would miss that too. The view from her apartment was not nearly so grand.

The apartment. Surely she wasn't going to spend her retirement years sitting in an apartment. She needed to be needed. What would it be like not to be responsible for anything or anybody? She spun back toward the clutter, dropping her hands to her sides at the sight of nearly 25 years' accumulation of papers, reports, supplies, file boxes, reference books, catalogs, brochures, record envelopes, and cardboard cartons. There were also a safe, a broken hat tree and a mixture of other valuable, worthless or unidentifiable litter.

"Tomorrow," she mused, "it will belong to the ages." She

tilted her head to read a pink phone message on her desk, scrunched it, and threw it near the overflowing wastebasket. "And ages is about how long it will take them to sort it all out," she added.

"Margaret," a soft voice intruded from the doorway. "Have you got a minute?" It was the boss's secretary, Mildred Adams, a slim, straight, black woman in her early 30s who had been with the agency ever since she was graduated from high school.

"Oh Millie, come on in." Margaret looked around. "Move those papers and you can sit there. No, put them over there. Or, no, here, give them to me.

"Now then," she continued once Millie was settled, "What can I do for you?"

"This is a little embarrassing, but Mr. Mann asked me to see if I can take over your job."

Margaret drummed her fingers on the edge of the desk and looked at the younger woman and smiled. "Oh you poor thing," she said. Both women laughed. "Now he starts thinking of a replacement." She looked at her watch. "I'm leaving in a few hours."

"Oh, I don't think I'm to be a replacement," Millie said. "I think I'm just supposed to keep things going for a little while."

Margaret shook her head. "Oh, that man," she said. "Well, I think I can at least show you how to dazzle Mr. Mann with footwork for a couple of days," she said, nudging an empty envelope box toward the file cabinet with slightly more force than necessary.

Millie sensed the tension. "Oh dear," she said, "It all seems so arbitrary, so unfair. When you're 65, they make you retire no matter how good a job you're doing."

Margaret raised her eyebrows. "I'm 74," she said simply. "They just think I'm 65." She gave Millie a mischievous grin. "But I keep the records. I could have stayed here until I was 90 if I'd wanted to."

Millie relaxed into her chair and began to laugh. "Age is a state of mind. And you're still too young to retire."

"No, it's time to retire," Margaret said. "Past time."

"What are you going to do? I suppose everyone asks you that."

"Yes they do. And I tell them I'm going to travel, probably do some volunteer work, and maybe take ballet lessons. I've always wanted to take ballet lessons."

Both women laughed. Then Margaret's tone changed. "I really don't have it figured out yet, Millie. I'll probably do some traveling. I'm certainly due. I never go anywhere -- hardly been outside of New York for ages. I'll go to Washington. I don't suppose that's really traveling, is it?"

"Oh, I don't know. Travel has more to do with where you go than how long it takes to get there. And Washington's a pretty place. Worth a trip."

Margaret swung her chair toward the window again, then back. "I want to visit my son's grave at Arlington. He was killed in Korea." She stared soberly far into the distance for a moment. "Then I'd like to go back to Cobblers Eddy, Indiana where I grew up."

"Where?"

Margaret seemed to snap out of her revere. "Cobblers Eddy, Indiana." she said. "It's a little itsy bitsy place no one has ever heard of."

"I've heard of it."

Margaret laughed. "Not very likely, Millie. It's sooo small. You would never have heard of it." She paused. "Oh my," she said, "how long has it been?" She thought for a moment. "It's been 58 years. Not once in all those years have I even heard the name of Cobblers Eddy mentioned. Not once. Why, it's not even on the map."

"But I did hear about it. Or read about it. Somewhere. Recently, too. Cobblers Eddy. I'm sure that's the name. Positive. It'll come to me."

"I wonder if it's still there," Margaret said. "It seemed awfully fragile. Not more than a couple of dozen houses. Barns right on the main road. If they widened the highway, the whole place could disappear."

As Millie watched the older woman, a trace of annoyance crept across her brow. "It's there. Believe me. I've heard of it. Honest."

"Did you really think I was only 65?" Margaret asked, tactfully changing the subject. "Why it's been nearly 60 years since I left Cobblers Eddy. If I do go out there, I suppose I'd best make some long distance calls first." She considered the idea for a moment. "*If* I go down there." She contemplated the idea briefly. "Who on earth would I call?" she wondered aloud. She glanced at Millie and sat up straight in her chair. "Well, that's neither here nor there, is it? Let's go to work."

She removed a fat, leather-bound account book from the shelf behind her and spread it out on top of the clutter that hid her desk. "This job is principally the processing of money and forms. Money in, money out; forms in, forms out," she said. She showed Millie how to keep the books straight, make out paychecks, and order supplies. And while she was doing it, her mind drifted back through the years to the sunny, hopeful days of her youth in a place called Cobblers Eddy.

Chapter Three

Cobblers Eddy, late Spring 1926

Some years before he died, Maggie's grandfather planted lilac bushes in rows at either side of the one-lane gravel road that the county built over the hill and down through the center of what was now her father's farm. By the spring of 1926, the mature bushes gave blossom to great puffs of lavender, their delicate aroma sweeping across the lush, green pastures below. As she reached the crest of the hill on her way home after slopping Mrs. Moss's pigs, Maggie's spirits were lifted by the perfume of her grandfather's sweet legacy.

In spite of her half hearted attempt to stay cool by rolling up her sleeves, Maggie's faded blue work shirt was darkened by small underarm crescents of perspiration. She rolled up the bottom hem of her tan, mid-thigh shorts. At the crest of the hill, she broke into an easy lope, her heavy work shoes kicking up scatterings of gravel as she glided down the hill. Maggie wasn't running because of any pressing need to get somewhere. She was running because she was young. And strong. And full of life and energy. And because the day sparkled with beauty and the promise of spring. And she was running because she just felt like it. And because it was downhill and easy. Her long yellow hair and broad shoulders moved in easy rhythm to her long, graceful strides.

As she strode down the road, she saw the lithe form of her friend Tom coming up the hill toward her. When he spotted her, he began to run toward her. When they met, Maggie expected Tom to turn around and stride down the hill with her. Instead, he ran on past her up the hill.

Maggie stopped. "Hey, you goofer," she shouted to him.

"Whoa," Tom said. He kept running in place, then ran backward until he was facing Maggie. She took a playful swipe at him with a full swing of her arm. Tom dodged away.

"I was just looking for you," Tom said.

"Well, you found me." She looked around. "Where's Alfie and Gordie?" she asked as they walked down the hill together.

"Doin' their chores, I suppose." Tom brushed the long, dark hair from his eyes. At 17, he was more sinewy than muscular — and very tanned, testimony to long and arduous hours spent on his father's farm.

"Tomorrow we're gonna have a picnic at Kocher's field. Can you come?" he asked.

"Before my chores?"

"You mean before you slop Mrs. Moss's pigs?"

Maggie bumped him with her hips, knocking him slightly off balance. "Well I didn't think you'd have a picnic before my morning chores."

"Sure, before you slop the pigs. We'll go down to Mrs. Moss's afterwards to help you with the sloppin'. Do you want me to bring a saddle?"

"What for?" Maggie asked. "You gonna ride Mrs. Moss's pigs now?"

"*I'm* not gonna ride anything. I thought *you* might wanna ride Kocher's cows."

Maggie was incredulous. "Tommm," she said, stretching out his name. "I'm not riding any cows."

"Why not?"

"Why should I?"

"We did."

"You mean *you* did. Alfie never rode a cow; neither did Gordie."

"Alfie's too small."

"Yeah, and Gordie's too big."

"Gordie was born too big," Tom said. They both laughed.

"But you're just the right size," Tom continued.

Maggie walked a few steps into the field at the side of the road just far enough to pull up a stalk of timothy hay. She stuck the stem end in her mouth. "Why don't *you* ride them again if you're so itchin' to see them ridden?"

"I already rode `em. `Sides, I'm too big now."

"Not for Echo, you're not too big," Maggie said over her shoulder as she turned off on the path toward her house.

Tom stopped. A twinkle came to his eye. "Neither are you," he shouted back as he resumed his way back up the hill.

Echo was a very large cow. Jim Kocher had considered her a real prize three years earlier when he traded half of his corn harvest for her at the 1923 state fair. She was only three months old then and already approaching the size of a full grown cow. By the time she was 18 months old and mature, she was nearly as tall at the shoulder as a work horse.

Jim Kocher's plan was to improve the quality of his herd by interbreeding Echo and her offspring with the rest of his herd. The normal way to improve a herd was to breed one's cows to a prize bull. But Jim Kocher thought he had a better idea. He could never hope to buy a prize bull, but Echo seemed destined to mother a superior brood — perhaps including a prize bull. And even if the prize breeding bull were not forthcoming, he would still have a great cow, and all her progeny. For a time, it looked as though he might be right. Echo grew into a creature of elegance, dignity, and beauty. Her straight back rose several inches above the other cows. Then one spring day, Jim Kocher put a lead clamp in Echo's nose and proudly led her up the dirt road, past the other farmers who waved with interest and, Jim thought, perhaps a bit of envy. They knew Echo was on her way to visit Kutch's bull.

But there were problems. It was nearly nightfall when Jim led Echo back. No waves of envy poured forth from the farms he passed. It seemed Kutch's bull was intimidated by Echo's size and lack of cooperation.

Echo made several more trips to other bulls before she was finally bred to a bull in Sizerville. The scrawny calf that resulted nine months later had to be hand fed because Echo had very little milk to give and even less interest in giving it. The woeful little calf was sold, and majestic Echo, her proportions unchanged by the experience of motherhood, continued to swagger among Jim Kocher's fat, unimpassioned herd. Her classic lines, nimble movements, and small bag of milk were in sharp contrast to the fat bellies, labored movements, and abundant dripping bags of the other cows.

Chapter Four

These days in early June were as near to perfection as days could get, Maggie thought as she peered, sleepy-eyed, out her bedroom window at the long morning shadows that dappled the lawn below. There was a light morning mist rising above the distant fields and a pleasant coolness to the air. It would be hot soon enough. She got dressed, brushed her teeth, and ran a comb rather carelessly through her long yellow hair — just enough to prevent any snarls. She would do a more complete job after her chores. A few minutes later, she was sitting on a three legged stool, her head propped against the plump belly of Daisy, one of her father's three milking cows. She squeezed two of Daisy's teats in easy rhythm, sending fine streams of milk pinging noisily into the white enamel pail she held clamped between her knees. Her father was milking one of the other cows while her mother was back at the house readying a hardy breakfast of ham, eggs and toasted homemade bread. As her father finished milking, Maggie picked up a small wicker basket and headed for the hen house. After she had collected the eggs and placed them in the cool dampness of the apple cellar to be candled later in the day, she returned to the house to clean up and join her parents for breakfast.

Now, finally, it was time to start the day.

Just before noon, Maggie tore off a piece of waxed paper from the Cut Rite roll and laid it neatly on the kitchen counter. She sliced two pieces of bread and some cold chicken to make herself a chicken, lettuce and mayonnaise sandwich, which she wrapped in the waxed paper and stuffed into a one quart berry basket. She removed the milk bucket from the ice box on the back porch and, after sniffing it to be sure it was still fresh, filled a one pint mason jar, then tore off another piece of waxed paper to use as a seal before screwing on the lid.

She broke off half a carrot, washed it in the sink and tucked it under the waxed paper that wrapped her sandwich.

"Okay," she thought aloud, "I'm ready."

A few minutes later, the three boys came around the side of the house. "Hey Maggie, you ready?" Tom called out.

"Just waitin' on you guys."

"If yer waitin' fer us, yer just wastin' your time," Gordie's deep voice drawled.

Maggie grabbed the jar and the basket from the counter. "See you later, Mom," she shouted over her shoulder, not waiting for a reply, which was just as well since her mother was working in the garden at the front of the house and didn't hear her anyway.

The four set out across the rolling fields of timothy and clover to the stone wall that separated Maggie's father's farm from Jim Kocher's. A sense of privacy prevailed there because of the way the hills came together. All the farm buildings and houses were blocked from view by trees, hedge rows and the natural slope of the countryside. The only possible intrusion would be from the train whose tracks wound around the hill. The bend was so sharp that the trains barely crept along. On the day Tom rode Old Man Kocher's Holsteins, heads appeared from both the engine and the caboose cheering him on. There would probably be no such riding today, however, because the cows were in another part of the pasture — a part too open to view.

So to Maggie's relief, the four lounged on a large rock in the shade of a mature maple tree surrounded by a hedge row. They ate their picnics leisurely, then ambled down to rinse their jars in the creek and set them on the big rock to dry.

Alfie and Gordie climbed to the top of the towering maple while Tom strolled out into the pasture to find a buttercup for Maggie.

"Come here, Maggie, I want to find out if you're going to heaven." He held the little yellow flower under Maggie's chin. "If this buttercup reflects under your chin, you go to heaven. If it doesn't, you go to the other place." He bent down to look up at Maggie's chin. "Oh-oh," he said.

"What do you mean 'oh-oh'?"

"No reflection."

"Give me that." Maggie grabbed the flower and held it under her own chin. "You weren't holding it close enough. There."

"Sorry. Still no reflection."

"Whaaat?" Maggie held the buttercup under her forearm. "See, there's a reflection on my arm. So there has to be one under my chin."

Tom took the buttercup back and held it under her chin again. "Sorry," he said. "You don't get to heaven by getting a reflection on your arm. Just under your chin." He returned her skeptical gaze with "It's hard to explain these things."

"Wait a minute, wait a minute." Maggie pulled the buttercup from his hand. "If it reflects under your chin, that means you like butter."

"Oh, is that what it means?" Tom shrugged. "Close enough."

"Close enough? Liking butter is close enough to going to heaven?" She sat, leaning against the trunk and put the buttercup through the top button hole in her shirt. Tom leaned against the trunk, and lowered himself so he was sitting very close to her. He then slid his arm around her waist.

Maggie looked at his hand clutching her waist. She looked away for a moment then looked Tom straight in the eye. "Are you trying to feel me up?" She said.

"No," Tom proclaimed, quickly removing his arm and sliding away. "No. Of course not."

"Then what were you doing?"

"Well, I guess I was snuggling. There's nothing wrong with snuggling, is there?"

Maggie didn't reply.

"Well, is there? You smell good. Like a flower. And I just

sort of snuggled up to you, that's all. Nothin' wrong with that."

"Come on, Tom. A flower? On a hot, sweaty day like today? My shirt's about soaked with sweat. Even weeds smell better than I do. Maybe you weren't feelin' me up, but you weren't far from it. And flowers have got nothing to do with it."

"Yes they do. Well, maybe not flowers, exactly, but I like the way you smell. It makes me want to snuggle."

Maggie lifted her arm and sniffed the moist crescent beneath it, then grimaced.

"Besides, Maggie, I would never feel you up."

"Ho ho. Not much, you wouldn't."

Just then, Topsy, the old hound dog that had attached herself to Maggie's family, waddled through the high grass, her tail whipping it as she came. "Come here, Topsy. Come on girl," Maggie called. The old dog ambled over and lay on her back sprawled across Maggie's lap. "She likes to have her belly scratched," Maggie said, rubbing Topsy's underside. "My goodness, Topsy girl, you've got a big ol' bloat bug on you. Two of 'em." Maggie began inspecting Topsy's underside and pulling off bloat bugs.

Then, after a moment and without looking up, she said, "What if I wanted you to?"

"Wanted me to what? Pick bugs off your dog?"

"No, what if I wanted you to feel me up?"

"Shhh. Maggie, keep your voice down." He looked up into the branches where Alfie and Gordie were, thankfully, high in the tree and obscured by the branches. "Holy smokes, Maggie, the things you say. I would never . . . Come on, Maggie, don't ask me questions like that. It's bad enough that you're so fetchin' . . . and you smell so good. You shouldn't be sayin' stuff like that."

"Well, would you?"

"Absolutely not." he said, adding after a moment, "I don't think so." He thought for a moment. "It wouldn't be right, you know. I don't guess it would." A few moments passed. "Maybe I would do it. Probably. Yeah, I guess I would." He still didn't look at her. "Yeah, I would," nodding his head vigorously. "Okay. For sure if you wanted me to."

"I thought so."

Tom looked straight ahead and Maggie continued searching through the fine hair on Topsy's belly. Neither spoke for an awkward moment.

"Well," Tom said, looking at her at last, "does that mean you want me to?"

"Of course not."

"Then why did you ask, for cryin' out loud?"

"Just wondered."

Tom got to his feet and sighed heavily. He picked up a small, flat stone and threw it low across Jim Kocher's field, watching it curve for a moment before dipping into the tall grass at the far end of the pasture.

"You're done," Maggie said as she dumped the contented dog from her lap. Topsy, casting a slightly annoyed backward glance, re-entered the tall grass, tail whipping as before.

"And speaking of smells," Maggie said climbing down from the rock, "it's time to slop Mrs. Moss's pigs."

Tom called up into the branches of the maple tree, "Come on, you guys, we've got some pigs to slop."

Two voices called back in unison, "Okay." Then Gordie's added, "We'll catch up to you."

As Maggie and Tom walked down the hill away from the tree, they met Jim Kocher's small herd of Holsteins grazing its way back toward Kocher's barn. In their midst was the high backbone and regal bearing of Echo.

Saying nothing, Tom looked at the cows, then caught Maggie's gaze. He raised his eyebrows and motioned toward the herd.

Maggie smiled broadly and tugged on Tom's arm. He bent toward her, thinking she was going to refuse again to ride one of the cows. Instead, she gave him a quick kiss on the cheek and, looking back to be sure she wasn't overheard, said, "I like the way you smell too." Then she turned abruptly and walked among the grazing cows, petting them lovingly as she did. She walked along side Echo and put her hand on the big cow's back. Echo began walking faster. Maggie kept up with her as she picked up speed. Soon the cow was walking faster and Maggie had broken into a slow jog. To keep up, she kept her hand lightly touching the cow's side. Then, to the boys' amazement, she reached to the top of Echo's back and, with both hands, tightly grabbed the loose leathery skin at the cow's shoulders and whooped, throwing herself on Echo's back. Echo stopped in her tracks, throwing Maggie's prone form farther forward than Maggie had intended. The cow put her head down and took short choppy jumps, swaying to and fro trying to dislodge Maggie. Tom watched flabbergasted as the large cow hopped and bucked awkwardly farther into the pasture with Maggie clinging to her back.

But Maggie was getting better situated. Using both hands, she grabbed loose skin high on Echo's neck and, clamping her legs at either side, shimmied back to a better balanced position. Finally, she grabbed onto the shoulder skin with just one hand and threw the other in the air, laughing and whooping as Echo bucked and swayed.

Alfie and Gordie saw her and joined Tom to catch up with the runaway Echo as the other cows scattered, unnerved by Echo's distress.

"How do I get off here?" Maggie called back to Tom.

"Just jump," he said. "But look out for the . . ."

She jumped.

"Cow plop," he finished.

Maggie got up and dusted herself off as the boys approached.

"Did you get any cow plop on you?" Tom asked, beginning to inspect her clothes.

Maggie gave him a quick elbow in the ribs, then started running toward Mrs. Moss's with all three boys in pursuit.

When she got to the railroad tracks, the slow moving train was blocking her path so, with barely a thought about it, she ran along side the train, grabbed the edge of the sliding boxcar door the same way she had grabbed Echo and, in one motion, flipped herself up and onto the floor of the empty boxcar.

This delighted the boys. They giggled and yahooed, increasing their paces until they caught up with the boxcar and each in turn flipped himself inside just as Maggie had done. Getting to their feet, Tom and Maggie started to do a somewhat wobbly Virginia Reel while Alfie imitated a banjo player strumming "Turkey in the Straw". Gordie laughed and danced by himself, then with Maggie, then with Tom, and soon all four were do-si-do'ing, spinning, elbow swinging, and stamping their feet to Alfie's musical beat.

The train began to pick up speed.

"Guess what, you guys," Maggie announced abruptly. "Unless you guys want to dance clear to New York City, this hoedown is over." She jumped out the open boxcar door, rolled on the ground, and looked up in time to see the three others jump out too.

She ran over to where the three boys were and found Tom and Gordie still laughing over the adventure, but Alfie was staring soberly into the distance.

"Alfie, what's the matter?" she asked. "Are you all right? Did you hurt yourself?"

"No, I'm okay. I just have a funny feeling."

"Oh oh, what's the matter?" Tom asked. "Is something wrong? Shall I get Dad?"

"No," Alfie said. "It was the jump. There's something really funny about that jump. It's really important."

"What?" asked Maggie. "The jump was important? Why?"

"Shhh," Tom said. "Wait a minute, Maggie. Let me handle this. That jump was important?"

Alfie seemed to be in a trance. Maggie had never seen him this way before.

"No. It's not that jump. It's another jump." He looked at Maggie. "It's your jump."

"My jump?" Maggie was surprised. "What was the matter with my jump?"

"I'm not sure. It's very confused. It's very sad," Alfie said, looking far into the distance. "Very, very sad. And really happy. But it didn't happen yet."

"Oh brother." Maggie said, looking over her shoulder at Tom.

Tom threw his hands in the air in a gesture of frustration. "Oh swell. What's that supposed to mean?"

Gordie watched in silence.

"What is this?" Maggie asked. "What's going on? Are you sure you're not hurt, Alfie? Get up and walk."

"No. I'm okay. Honest. I can walk okay. It's just that I had this funny feeling."

Maggie looked at Tom again.

"The preacher says that Alfie is — what's the word, Alfie?"

"Sensitized."

"Yeah, sensitized. He sees things that nobody else can see."

"Actually, I don't `see' them either. I just sort of feel `em," Alfie said.

"And most of the time, he's right," Tom said.

"All the time," Alfie corrected.

Tom tossed his head. "Yeah, right. You're always right because nobody can understand what the heck you said."

Maggie was watching the two brothers. "You mean Alfie knows things that haven't happened yet?"

"Yeah."

"And Alfie knows they're going to happen?"

"Sometimes."

"Aw come on you guys. That's spooky," Maggie said. "Alfie can tell the future? I'm having a hard time swallowing that one."

"Now look, Maggie — and you too Gordie — I don't care if you believe it or not, you got to promise you won't tell a soul about this. Especially not Mom and Dad. They don't want us tellin' anyone about Alfie's, ahh . . ."

"Sensitivity," Alfie volunteered. He seemed fully recovered.

"Right. Most people just don't understand. Now let's go slop us some pigs."

The four young people headed across the fields toward the village of Cobblers Eddy. Maggie hung back, knowing Tom would follow suit. She wanted to talk with him privately.

"Tom, that was really strange. I never saw Alfie act like that before. Does he do it often?"

Tom was uncomfortable. "No. Not very often." He pulled out a stalk of timothy and stuck the stem in his mouth, glad for an excuse to have his mouth occupied. He could still talk, of course, but the timothy seemed to make it less easy.

Maggie persisted. "Tell me about it."

Tom pulled out another stalk of timothy and tried to

stick it in Maggie's mouth.

She pushed it away. "Tell me," she said.

"You already know about all there is to tell. Mom and Dad really don't like us to talk about it."

"Why not?"

"I don't know. It's my dad, mostly. He doesn't like the mumbo jumbo." He looked at Maggie and smiled self consciously. "I guess it's not the way he likes things to be. He wants them more simple. Calmer. He doesn't want to become known as the father of the boy wonder who sees and hears things that no one else can."

They walked in silence for a while. Tom hoped it was the end of that topic. He would have changed the subject, but at the moment, he couldn't think of anything to say.

"What kind of things?" Maggie asked, "What kind of things does Alfie see and hear?"

"Oh that. Well, he doesn't see things. Not with his eyes. He sort of feels them — and sometimes he hears them. He knows things he couldn't know — like things that haven't happened yet. And he hears all kinds of stuff. Like funny sounds coming from things. And it always means something even though most of the time he doesn't know what. Boy, Maggie, you better not tell a soul about this. My dad would get so mad, I just hate to think about it. This is our family's biggest secret. Even my dad's brothers don't know about it."

"I won't tell, Tom. Honest I won't. I won't let it slip out, either."

They walked in silence for a while.

"What kind of things has he known about?"

"Geez, Maggie. Don't keep askin' me."

"I gotta know, Tom. I won't tell anybody, but I gotta know. I'm part of whatever it was he felt back there in the field. He said it was my jump that was important. I've got a right to know."

"He knows when supper's ready."

"C'mon, Tom. Lots of folks know when supper's ready."

"But he knows all the time. Every day. Within a minute. No matter where he is. No matter how much my mother is off schedule."

Tom looked at Maggie. She didn't seem convinced.

"My dad got a flat tire on the concrete road last week. I was with him. When he went to fix it, he found there was no jack. Someone had taken it out of the car at home and forgotten to put it back. Along comes Alfie on horseback with the jack. How'd he known?"

"What did your father say?"

"He got mad. He said we could have walked home to get the jack. An' he yelled at Alfie for taking a chance that people would guess his secret."

Tom continued: "He's always doin' stuff like that. Remember that kid, what was his name? The one that almost drowned last winter? What was his name?"

"You mean Bobbie LaRue? Fell through the ice? Your father arrived in the nick of time and pulled him out."

"Right. Do you remember who was with my dad?"

"No."

"Alfie. He and Dad were ridin' along a mile or two from the pond and all of a sudden Alfie starts screamin' that Bobbie LaRue fell through the ice. So my dad turns around and steps on the gas. And all the time Alfie is saying, `Hang on Bobbie. We're comin', Bobbie. Hang on.' And when they talked to Bobbie later, he said he thought he was a goner because no one saw him fall in. But do you know what else he said?"

Maggie bit her lower lip and stared at Tom.

"He said he could hear a voice telling him to hang on." Tom said.

A shiver went up Maggie's spine. She let out a long, low whistle and looked ahead at Alfie, who seemed terribly small and ordinary walking next to the considerable bulk of Gordie. "Golly," was all she could say.

"Can you imagine what Alfie's life would be like if people knew?" Tom asked.

"Golly."

Chapter Five

A broad smile spread across Maggie's face as she approached the white clapboard house that was home to her parents and her. Her thoughts were not of Alfie and his "sensitivity," but rather of Tom. She liked him a lot. And she knew very well he liked her back. She kept thinking about how she had tricked him into admitting he'd like to feel her up when she was sure that wasn't really what was on his mind. "Not nice of me," she breathed out loud, then laughed at the memory. It wasn't very often Tom got flustered, but he sure did today, she thought. Certainly she was as attracted to him as he was to her, but girls had to be careful. "One of these days," she sighed. "But not now."

Topsy waddled out from the rear of the house and sniffed Maggie's shoe briefly, wagged her tail, and waddled back.

Feeling comfortably mellow, Maggie ambled up the steps to the front porch and opened the screen door and almost let it slam, catching it at the last moment and easing it shut, as her father had been admonishing her to do for as long as she could remember.

She could hear her father's excited voice trumpeting in the kitchen. "Lots of folks are well off," he was saying. She was startled. He usually didn't speak so loudly. She stopped and listened. "I suppose we're well off for that matter. I'm talking real money. Honest to gosh really, enormously wealthy. I mean filthy, filthy rich. Rich enough that we could buy off the mortgage on this farm and flat out buy every other farm in and around Cobblers Eddy. And never feel a dent in our fortune."

Maggie could see her mother bending over the sink peeling potatoes as her father paced behind her.

"You'll get used to it. You'll love it. You know there's a great big park right smack in the middle of New York. Rolling fields, and fountains, and even a zoo. And, you'll make friends. We'll all make friends."

As Maggie entered the room, both parents turned their gazes toward her. The conversation stopped abruptly, followed by a moment of awkward silence.

Her mother recovered first. "Oh hello, Dear," she said. "Did you bring back the jar and the basket from your lunch?"

Maggie snapped her fingers. "Darn. We were going to stop for them on our way back from Mrs. Moss's. I'll get them tomorrow."

"Remember," her mother said, "I use them for canning. They don't grow on trees."

"The jars, you mean."

"Right, Dear."

"Not the baskets."

"No, Dear," she smiled sweetly.

Maggie got a paring knife out of the drawer. "Want some help?" she said.

"I think that's enough potatoes," her mother said. "But you could cut up the string beans."

There was another moment of silence. Then Maggie spoke: "Ah, have you two by chance got anything you might want to tell me?"

Her parents looked at each other. "About what, Dear?" her mother asked.

"About being filthy rich, living in New York, and buying all the farms around Cobblers Eddy including the mortgage on this one, which, I think, we already own outright."

Her mother smiled pleasantly again and her father laughed out loud and said, "Don't get your hopes up, Sweetheart. It's not definite. A couple of things have to come together just right."

Her mother said, "Your father has an opportunity to make a very large amount of money in New York, but it will mean mortgaging the farm and moving there."

"Mortgage the farm?" Maggie's tone was incredulous. "Who'd run it if we were in New York?"

"Oh we'd find someone to lease it to, Maggie. But nothing is certain yet," her father said.

"You can't lease this farm to some strangers. I love this place." She wrinkled her nose in distaste.

"Maggie, calm down," her father said. "You look like you just ate a bug."

But Maggie did not calm down. Her eyes moistened and her voice trembled. "You can't just decide to mortgage this farm and move away. How about us? How about me? I was born here. You were born here. Just the other day, you were going to remodel this house. Now you're going to mortgage it, land and all? Who's going to live here? How are you going to get it back? What if they don't want to move off it? Someone else living on our farm."

Now her father lost his good humor. "That's about enough of that, Maggie. You don't know what's at stake. And until you do, I'll thank you not to make judgments. I already said it's not definite."

"I don't want to be rich. I want to stay here."

"Oh, this is just great," her father said in disgust. "Life is not just about you and what you want, Maggie." He walked toward the door. "Sometimes it's about what other people want. What they've trained for and put off for all too long." Then to Maggie's mother, "Call me when supper's ready, I'll be down candling eggs." He walked abruptly out the front door. The screen door slammed behind him.

Maggie leaned into her mother and began to cry softly.

Her mother put her arm around her. "It's been a long time coming, Maggie. But this is what your father has been preparing for all his life." She used the dish towel dry her hands then dabbed Maggie's tears.

The screen door slammed again. Maggie's father reappeared and made a bee line to the closet to get an egg basket. He looked at the mother and daughter clinging to each other. "Oh brother," he lamented on his way back out. The screen door slammed again.

Finally, Maggie pulled away and resumed cutting up the string beans. "If he's been planning it for so long, how come this is the first I've heard of it?"

"That's a very good question," her mother said. "I don't really know. I suppose it just never came up." She put the peeled potatoes in a pan, filled it with water and put it on the hottest part of the stove to boil, then put the potato peels in a bread pan. "Do you want to take these down to Mrs. Moss's tomorrow?"

"Thanks."

"Don't forget to bring back the bread pan."

"I won't."

They continued to prepare dinner in silence for a few minutes, then Maggie's mother spoke.

"Have you ever wondered why your father never went into the business he studied in college?"

"I thought he did. Insurance. He sells insurance as well as running the farm."

"Oh, that's nothing. The extra money's nice of course, but it's more of a hobby than anything. A substitute. He studied high finance. The kind they do in New York. Investments — stocks and bonds, that sort of thing. And, according to the Comstock brothers, he was an absolute whiz."

"The Comstock brothers?"

"Yes, you've seen them. They stop by every so often. Your daddy went to school with them. In fact, they're the ones who arranged for him to go to New York."

Maggie stopped cutting and looked at her mother. "They're the ones who want Daddy to mortgage the farm?"

"Oh, no, no. That was his idea. They wanted to loan him the money, but he insists on using his own."

"There must be a better way than mortgaging the farm."

"Honey, mortgaging the farm is an excellent idea. He'll lease the land to local farmers, rent the house, and take out a mortgage on the whole thing. It's all reversible, if we — or you, perhaps — ever want to reclaim the farm.

"Someone else will be living in our house," Maggie said, almost to herself.

"And the rent and leasing will pay for the mortgage. That's what your father says. Will you set the table, Dear?"

Maggie took three plates out of the cupboard. "I can't believe this. You actually want to move off the farm and go to New York City?"

"Oh, heavens, no. I dread the move. I've dreaded it for years and years. I have no idea what I'll do in New York City."

"Then why . . ."

"Your poor father. He studied business finance at the Wharton School in Philadelphia. He was valedictorian of his class. After he was graduated, we got married and while we were on our honeymoon, his father — your grandfather — had a stroke. So your father stayed around here to take care of him and run the farm. Then days tumbled into months and years. And then you were born and Grandpa died, your father wanted you to know what farm life was like, and there was his insurance business and, with one thing or another, we just stayed."

"Then why are we moving now? And why so sudden?"

"The Comstocks. Instead of offering to loan him the money, they arranged to get a mortgage on the farm to provide the money he needs to get started. They also found a brownstone in New York."

"What's a brown stone?"

"It's a house — a spiffy New York house made of big brown stones. Your father says ours . . ."

"Ours. We have a house in New York?"

"Yes. The Comstocks found it. Your father says it has five floors and no yard . . ."

"No yard? We have a house in New York with no yard?"

"I guess so. Your father says it has a little patio in the back, but no grass. Anyway, he says it has lots of brass doorknobs, and gold leaf trim and high ceilings and chandeliers.

"Let me get this straight. This move might not happen but the Comstocks went and bought a five story house made of brown stone for Daddy anyway."

"I don't think they've bought it yet."

"But they will if the job goes through."

"Sounds like they expect it will."

She sighed. "I guess. Anyway. It still might not. The mortgage on the farm hasn't actually come through yet. The Comstocks have to get it approved then your dad has to sign it and it has to be registered by the end of the company's fiscal year . . . "

"What's a physical year?"

"Fiscal year. I don't know what it means but it's the end of June. You'll have to ask your dad about that."

"That soon? Are you hoping it'll all fall through?

"Oh no. Your father deserves his chance. Oh, Lord, if anyone ever deserved it, he does. Have you ever thought how much of his life he was given to other people? Your grandfather, me, you, all of us. If you ever wonder why I love your father so very much... He's the most kind, self-less man who ever walked the earth. I'd do anything in this world to make him happy."

Neither spoke for a time. Maggie was lost in thought as she finished setting the table and scooped the cooked beans into a serving dish. Her mother mashed the potatoes and turned over the sausages one last time.

"He really stayed on the farm for us, didn't he?" Maggie said at last. "For me really. So I could grow up on a farm instead in a big city."

"Yes Dear, and for your grandfather too."

"I didn't know he'd been planning this for so long."

"Yes, Dear. Will you call your father for supper?"

"I think I'll go down to tell him."

Her mother looked at her wearily. "Just don't be long. This isn't a good time for one of your heart to hearts. Supper'll get cold."

Maggie was out the door.

She found her father sitting on an upturned crate candling eggs over an inverted coffee can with an electric light inside and an oval shaped hole in the top. It was a rudimentary contraption fashioned years earlier by Maggie's grandfather when the farm was first electrified. The light shined through the egg, revealing any blood spots. There was nothing wrong with the few blood spot eggs that turned up, but they could be very off-putting to unsuspecting people who bought them at the store. So they were put aside and used instead at home.

"Supper's ready," Maggie said.

Her father turned to see her silhouetted in the doorway. "I'm just about done."

Maggie walked over and put her hand on his shoulder.

"I'm sorry Daddy. I didn't understand."

He looked up from the candling light and put his hand briefly on hers. "That's all right, Sweetheart."

"Mom explained the whole thing to me. I had no idea . . ."

Her father put the last egg in the carton and placed a light protective piece of cardboard on top. "I was going to tell you all about it." He turned off the candling light and stood. "I just wanted to be sure it was really going to happen first. Did your mother tell you that it might not happen at all if the mortgage isn't approved on time?"

"June 30th, she said."

"I didn't want you to hear it the way you did. It's really good news, you know — not bad news."

Maggie's mother was now silhouetted in the doorway. "Come on you two. Supper is ready and getting cold."

Maggie and her father laughed. "Was a time — yesterday, I think — when you'd just have called me from the porch. Now two of you come down."

"I was afraid you and Mag would get to talking . . ."

"Probably would have. I was just about to tell her what a good thing this move could be for us."

The three of them walked, arm in arm, back up to the house.

Maggie's father was a slim, sinewy man who radiated energy. He put some ketchup on his sausage, then rubbed his hands together and looked first at Maggie's mother, then at Maggie. "Okay," he said. "Here's the way it is. People in New York are making huge fortunes on the stock market. They are people with very little money of their own and people who know a lot less than I do about investing. And people who lack the connections I have in New York, thanks to my friends the Comstocks.

"Now here's what our choices are: We can keep what money we now have tied up in this farm and work the farm for the rest of our lives. Or we can mortgage the farm — at a very favorable rate, I might add — and join the Comstocks in New York. The mortgage money from the farm would give us so much money to put on margin in the market, that we could easily make several times the value of the farm in just a few months.

"Maggie, you could go to any school you wanted. Within

a year or two, I could pay off the mortgage. Probably add to the acreage in the process. We could go to Europe. Your children, Maggie, could be born into a wealthy family and have all the advantages. We could *be* something."

"But mortgage the farm? Rent out the house and the barn and the chicken house? What if something went wrong? What if we couldn't get it back?" Maggie asked.

"Relax, Sweetheart. There are virtually no risks. The world could explode. This boom that's been going on in New York could suddenly stop the moment we hit town. I could come down with a severe case of the stupids and forget everything I know and we'd still be okay. The farm would still be ours. Also, I have a lot of faith in the Comstocks. They were my best buddies in school. And in the years since we were graduated — years I've spent here on the farm — they've been making it big in New York. Now they're incredibly rich. They wouldn't let anything happen to us. Besides, nothing is going to happen to us. Nothing bad, anyway."

"What about your insurance business? What would happen to that?"

"Someone else would handle that. And I'd continue to get a small commission from it. And that, too, would help pay the mortgage. But that's not what's important."

Maggie listened to her father carefully and tried to make sense of it. But her thoughts kept coming back to Cobblers Eddy and the friends she had there. "We could come back here for a visit?" she asked.

"Sure."

"Could we bring people from here up to New York?"

Here father cocked an eyebrow. "Like who?" he said. "As if I didn't know."

"Well, not just Tom alone. Alfie and Gordie would come with him."

"I don't see why not. I think we could put them all up."

"Hmm. It takes some getting used to, doesn't it? I mean the idea. You know what I mean." She looked longingly around the room again.

Her father smiled warmly. "Yes, it does. And it might not happen at all. Timing is critical. I have to get a document signed in New York, then sign it here in Cobblers Eddy, and file it with the courts before the end of the fiscal year, midnight, June 30. And there are half a dozen things that could happen in New York — things I have no control over — things that could prevent it from happening at all. Keep your fingers crossed, Sweetheart." He patted her hand lovingly. "I was going to wait until it was certain before telling you so you wouldn't be disappointed. Now I'm glad I didn't wait."

Chapter Six

"Ma, do you think I could borrow Eldon's slacks?" Gordie called from upstairs.

His mother was downstairs in the kitchen ironing his father's pants. "Ask Eldon," she called back.

Gordie came down the stairs and peeked around the doorway. "I can't. He's making a run with Guy Cragel's hay truck."

"Oh yeah," she looked over her glasses at her youngest son, who was wearing a longsleeved dress shirt but no pants. She gave him a long wolf whistle. "Great legs," she said without expression, then exchanged the iron she was using for a freshly heated one from the stove top. "Eldon's pants won't fit you anyway," she said.

"That's the problem. Nobody's pants fit me. But Eldon's come the closest." Gordie straddled a chair, resting his chin on his hands across the back of it.

"What's the matter with yours?" his mother asked.

"Too short."

"But we just got them."

"I know," he said. "I'm a growing boy."

"Land sakes," his mother said without looking up from her ironing. "You are that." She thought for a moment. "Maybe I could let them down a little bit in the legs. Is there any more material left?"

"I don't know. I'll get them." He bounded up the stairs and came back with a pair of light blue trousers.

His mother held them upside down before her and looked at the inside of one pants leg. "There's a little," she said.

"Can you let them down?"

"Under one condition."

"What?"

"That you stop growing."

As she tore out the hem stitching, Gordie called to her again, this time from the pantry, "Ma, can I borrow Pa's razor, do you think?"

"What on earth for?"

"To shave off my whiskers."

"You don't have any whiskers."

Gordie came into the kitchen. "Yes I do, Ma," he said.

"Where?"

"Here." He fingered his chin.

His mother stepped up close to him and squinted. "Where?"

"Right here. Here, let me have your hand." He rubbed her middle finger against his chin. "See? Feel that?"

"Oh yeah. In fact, when the light's just right, you can actually see it. But you don't need no razor." She went back to her ironing. "Just put a dab of milk on it and let the cat lick it off."

"Ahh, c'mon, Ma." Gordie went back to the pantry.

"Go ahead. Use your pa's razor. But don't cut yourself." She spread the pants on the ironing board. "Lather your face up with soap first."

"I know, Ma."

"An' clean off the razor. Don't leave your pa with a dirty razor."

"Okay."

"You might want to strop the razor a couple of times, too. As soon as your pa comes in from the fields, he's going to want to get ready too."

"Okay, Ma. Ouch."

"Cut yourself, didn't y'? Your pa don't cut himself."

"My pa don't have a face full o' pimples."

After a few minutes, Gordie came out of the pantry patting his face with a towel.

"Let me see," his mother said.

Gordie pulled the towel away from his face.

"Hmmm," his mother dead panned, "I hope you heal

before the strawberry social tonight."

Gordie went into the pantry again where his mother could hear him rummaging around.

"Ma, where do we keep the shoe polish?" he called.

"Land Sakes alive! What would you be wantin' with shoe polish?" she called back.

"Shine my shoes."

"Your work shoes?"

"The only shoes I got."

"You're going to polish your work shoes?"

"Never mind, I found it."

His mother smiled to herself as she ironed his trousers. "He's going to polish his work shoes," she murmured.

"Ma, where is the — never mind, I found it."

"The what?"

"The Vaseline. But I found it."

She folded his pants and took them to him in the pantry. He was splashing water on his hair.

"Ah," she said, "now it's all clear. You're washing your hair in Vaseline, right?"

"No. Combing it."

"Of course," she said.

He took a dab of Vaseline, rubbed it in his hands and then into his wet hair. Then, looking in the mirror, he used a comb to make a part in the front of his hair. When he was done, he looked at his mother again and said, "How do I look?"

She looked him up and down, squinted, then threw his pants at him. "Put these on and I'll tell you," she said.

He put on his pants.

"They're a little snug in the waist," she said.

"They'll be okay for tonight."

"Your legs pop out a little at the bottom."

"Not as much as they did before you fixed 'em." He ran upstairs and returned wearing a belt with his pants.

"So how do I look?" he asked again.

She smiled, then walked up to the towering teenager and gave him a hug. "You look like a son who's going to make his ma proud," she said. Then, holding him at arms length, she added, "Maybe we could give those trousers to Eldon and get you a new pair from the catalog. Extra large."

"That'd be nice . . . if Eldon don't mind wearin' his younger brother's hand me downs."

"Bah," she said with a wave of her hand. "He don't care. He'd still be gettin' a pair of pants he didn't have before." She pulled a kitchen chair away from the table. "Sit down for a second, Son. I want to finish combing your hair. You only got the front of it combed."

He sat while she ran his part the rest of the way back to the crown of his head, then fussed over it a little.

"Who's the lucky girl?" she asked matter of factly.

Even the back of Gordie's neck got red as he blushed. "Ah, Ma, there don't have to be no girl, just because I got dressed up."

"It's not Maggie, is it?"

"Nah. Maggie's Tom's girl. An' my friend."

"Then who?"

"I don't know. Maybe . . . nah. I don't know. I was just thinkin' . . . if I met Gloria Baggins there, I might . . . well, I might at least want to look good."

"Well, you do look that, son. You do look good."

When Gordie's hair was finished, he stood up again and his mother returned to her ironing. "The Baggins must have 25 kids. Which one is she?"

"They have 14. She's the pretty one with the long, blonde hair."

"A whole bunch of them have long blonde hair — even the boys. Which one is she?"

"Her hair is lighter than any of the others'. And she has sort of a deep voice."

"You mean Froggie?"

Gordie sat down again. "Don't call her that, Ma. Her name is Gloria."

His mother stole a quick glance at him. "Gloria," she corrected herself. "She's a lucky girl to have my handsome son sweet on her."

"Shucks Ma, I didn't say I was sweet on her or nothin'." Gordie continued to sit, staring at the floor.

"I'm sorry I called her Froggie, Son. I wasn't thinkin'."

"Oh, that's okay. Everyone calls her Froggie because her voice is like crackley and deep. But it ain't fair. She can't help it. And there's a lot more to her than her voice." He paused as if considering his words carefully, then added, "An' I like her." He squinted one eye at his mother and added, "But that don't mean I'm sweet on her."

His mother gave him a kiss on the top of his neatly combed hair. It tasted like Vaseline.

Chapter Seven

The strawberry social was the prime rite of spring in Cobblers Eddy. Plump, juicy red strawberries were easy to cultivate and among the season's first fruits to ripen. Somewhere on virtually every property in and around Cobblers Eddy, there was a strawberry patch. Even Mrs. Moss had one tucked away a safe distance from the pigs. Strawberries were tasty, colorful, plentiful and could be made into a host of pies, shortcakes, jams, dressings, ice creams, puddings and tarts.

The ground was still wet with dew when Tom and Alfie picked six quarts of strawberries from the garden so their mother could make strawberry tarts. She believed that one of the secrets to her tarts was the freshness of the strawberries. Each year she made them more fancy and, she thought, more tasty. And each year she drew more compliments on them. To no one's surprise, when it was time to go to the strawberry social, she carried the tarts out to the car herself in a large basket and cuddled them on her lap in the front seat during the brief, bumpy ride to the church, even though there was ample room in the back with Tom and Alfie.

The boys' father pulled the car up to the parking area alongside the sprawling church lawn. There were no other cars. He put on the emergency brake, got out of the car and took a few steps toward the church, then returned to the car to open the door for his wife. "Well, here we are once again," he said, "the only people here. Where is everybody?"

"I don't know," Alfie said, as he and Tom followed their mother out of the car.

"Every year, we're the first ones here," their father continued. "What time does this thing start?"

"When everybody gets here," Alfie and Tom chimed in together. They laughed because that was the time every social event started in Cobblers Eddy. And their father could never quite adjust to it. He was always prompt, always the first one there, and he always began by wondering where everybody else was.

He walked to the church, opened the door and stuck his head in. "Nobody there, either." he said.

"Some good elves must have set up the tables, then went back into the forest," the boys' mother said.

The other three looked at her blankly. Her husband let out a faint sound of pain. Her frequent flights of fairytale fantasy were sometimes a source of embarrassment to her husband and sons.

"You're a little early," a voice came from the hill below. It was Marion, a heavy, busy woman in a white apron who did volunteer work for the church. She was walking briskly, puffing, toward the church. "Just went down to the house to get cleaned up a bit," she explained between deep breaths.

"What time does this thing start, anyway?" the boys' father shouted across the lawn to her.

"When everybody gets here," she said as she disappeared through the church door.

He shrugged. "Well, might as well unload the car and put our stuff on the tables," he said.

"Strawberry tarts," his wife corrected. "Not stuff."

"Yes," he said.

Folks from in and around Cobblers Eddy materialized in fits and starts. Their arrivals seemed almost accidental. Typically, three people in a cluster stood about a hundred feet down the road talking and holding their contributions to the social. After a few minutes, they headed slowly toward the church lawn where they placed their food and packages on a table, then talked a bit more before slowly unwrapping them.

There was an engaging sense of timelessness in Cobblers

Eddy. Except for Tom's father, no one seemed to hurry. No one made an entrance. People just suddenly were there. Some came from across the concrete road, some walked through the fields, others emerged from the back of the lawn, and still others came out the church door without having seemed to go in it first. Social events sprang to life effortlessly in Cobblers Eddy — as if they had lives of their own. No one seemed to be in charge.

Gordie was there as was Gloria Baggins. And so were both their families. Gordie's mother was right; all the Baggins did look alike with their lithe bodies and long, pale hair — even the boys. Only Buck and Blanche Baggins, the parents, bore no resemblance to each other or to their 14 children — all of whom were in attendance.

Mrs. Baggins was a big bosomed, broad shouldered woman of considerable physical power. She didn't take care of her children as much as she orchestrated them, using hand movements, nods of the head, clearing of the throat and terse verbal instructions to maintain control.

Her husband, who was small and wiry, looked perpetually angry. He had a full head of reddish gray hair which he pushed straight back. His wild, heavy eyebrows were angled in a way that accentuated his look of anger. He paid scant attention to his children and none whatsoever to his wife.

Buck Baggins was a contradiction. On one hand, he was country poor and disorganized. He had more children than he could responsibly raise. And he had at least four hound dogs for each child. His house was in ill repair and his weed strewn yard was punctuated by rusted wagons, parts of automobiles, broken ice boxes, tires, chains, discarded furniture and other twisted junk.

But Buck Baggins knew more about all things mechanical — particularly the internal combustion engine — than anyone else in four counties.

As was typical of him at such gatherings, he spent the evening of the strawberry social leaning against the trunk of an apple tree explaining the workings of a tractor gear box to an audience of five men who hung on his every word. Occasionally he called to one of his children to bring him some food or a cold drink so as not to interrupt the flow of his impromptu clinic.

When he called out, "Hey, Froggie, bring me something wet, will ya'? Yer old man's about thirstin' to death," he got a surprise. A gentle teenage voice called back, "Sir, her name is Gloria."

Buck Baggins's wild eyebrows dipped precipitously at the bridge of his nose. His face turned red and his nostrils flared. "Who said that?" he demanded in a voice loud enough to quiet other conversations.

"I did, Sir," came the voice.

"Come here," he demanded.

The gargantuan form of Gordie slunk into view. When Buck saw the size of the owner of the voice, his anger doubled.

"Who the hell are you?" he spat.

"I'm . . . "

"And, who in hell do you think you are telling me what my own kid's name is?"

By now, there were no other conversations going on at the strawberry social. Everyone in Cobblers Eddy and everyone who lived on any of the surrounding farms was focused, full attention, on the angry man with the red face and the huge teenager he was berating.

"Her name is Gloria, Sir."

"How'd you like a whippin', boy? You think you're too big to get whipped?"

"No."

"Well, you're not. You're just a big, stupid kid buttin' in where you're not wanted and where you got no business."

"Sir, I don't want to start no argument. But no one has the right to call her Froggie. She is a lot more than her voice. She has a beautiful name and, by rights, she ought to be called by it."

Buck looked at Gordie sideways, squinting one eye as he did. "What are you sayin' boy?"

"Nobody oughta call Gloria 'Froggie'. Most especially not her own pa who's supposed to love her. That's all I got to say. 'Cept I didn't mean to cause a ruckus, an' I'm sorry for that."

There was a moment, perhaps ten seconds, of awkward silence. Then Buck spoke again in a somewhat conciliatory voice. "Well, that's all right, Boy. As long as you're sorry for causin' a ruckus. An' I usually do call her," he paused, "Gloria. It's just sometimes I slip." He looked at his daughter, "Gloria, honey, will you get your daddy a drink of fruit juice?" He glanced at Gordie as if for approval, then looked away. "Now where was I?" he said.

"You was just talkin' about gettin' into the gear box proper," a voice from the crowd said.

Gloria brought her father a glass of fruit juice which he took without missing a beat in his narrative. Then she walked over to Gordie and led him away from the group.

"You know . . . " she said in her deep, gravelly voice. She walked a few more steps before continuing. "You're not nearly as shy as I thought you were." She pushed her face against Gordie's sleeve to muffle her laughter. "I can't believe you said that to him. I will have a picture of his face in my brain forever. Nobody talks to him that way. Ever. No one. He has a face like a hatchet and a temper to match. He could scare a charging bull into turning tail." She buried her head in his sleeve again and laughed and laughed. Gordie began to laugh too. He felt awfully good.

Like everyone else at the social, Maggie watched the exchange between Gordie and Buck Baggins. She was mildly surprised at Gordie's ability to handle himself. But her attention was still on her father's revelation. The possibility of moving to New York City did not yet seem real. She had expected to stay in Cobblers Eddy forever. Her mind began to swim when she tried to picture living anywhere else. But, New York City — that was far away to the extreme.

She found herself watching Alfie and Gordie throughout the evening, wondering if she should tell them. And wondering if Alfie might already know. If he did, he gave no sign.

She had just about decided to tell Tom when the argument broke out between Buck and Gordie. Now, as Gordie and Gloria Baggins walked away, Maggie turned her gaze toward Tom, who lifted his eyebrows and motioned toward Gordie and Gloria.

"Let's get some shortcake," Maggie said.

"Okay." Tom got to his feet and held her hand briefly, then quickly let go as they walked to the shortcake table.

"That was kinda interesting," Tom said. "The little old guy threatens to beat up the young big guy. And the big guy, who is a little slow talkin', talks him down."

Maggie didn't respond. Tom walked with her a bit. "You just don't see that every day."

Maggie kept walking slowly but didn't answer him.

"Actually, you don't even see that every week."

No response from Maggie.

"Once a month perhaps, but you re-e-e-ally have to keep your eyes open." He looked at her faraway gaze. "Maggie," he said with emphasis. "What are you thinking about? You're a million miles away."

She looked at him. "Oh, Tom," she said. "I feel like I'm going a million miles away."

"What do you mean?"

"Let's get some shortcake, first. This is kinda private. Maybe we can eat it on the bench over there by the church. Then I can tell you."

Tom cut two pieces of cake and put them on saucers, then Maggie dripped chopped strawberries and syrup over them. They moved to the bench where Maggie sat down and Tom straddled the bench facing her.

"Tell me," Tom said.

"Oh Tom, I might be going to New York with my mom and daddy."

"When?"

"In a month or two."

"How long are you going to be gone?"

An expression of surprise flashed across Maggie's face. "Forever, Tom. We might be moving to New York. For. Ever."

Tom smiled broadly. "Come on, Maggie. That's crazy."

"It's true, Tom. I mean it. My dad might get a job there."

"Why would he do that to you? You belong here. That would be awful." He looked at the ground for a moment as if searching for a way to express himself. "That's about the worst thing I can think of. Gosh, that's stupid. Why would he ever want to go to New York City, for cryin' out loud?"

"He's always wanted to go to New York City. Even when

he was a child, Mom says. He once planned to work on Wall Street."

Tom was dumbfounded. "He even knew what street he wanted to work on?"

"Wall Street is a place, not a street, silly. It's New York's sort of money center. People sell stocks and bonds there." She knew Tom wasn't going to understand. "Stocks and bonds are like ownership shares of companies and things."

"Why can't he sell them here — like he sells insurance?" Tom asked.

"Oh Tom. How can I say it? Daddy's always wanted to go to New York. He even studied for it. I never dreamed he'd actually do it."

"Humph, I'll bet he had to do a whole lot of studying to sell things in New York," Tom said sarcastically.

"He did," Maggie said. "After college, he went to a special school in Philadelphia, the Wharton School, and studied and won awards. He got a degree there, too. He came out at the top of his class. Why, his classmates have been trying to get him to New York ever since."

"Then why did he come back here to sell insurance?"

"Because my grandpa got sick and died, that's why. And Daddy had to come back here to take care of the farm and things. If Grandpa hadn't got sick and died, Daddy'd be in New York right now. And so would my mom and I. I'd be a city girl."

Maggie had never thought of it in quite those terms before. She was a country girl only because her grandfather had died, leaving the responsibilities of the farm to her father.

Tom was silent. He looked at the ground. "You said it's just a possibility, didn't you? It hasn't happened yet, has it?"

"No, but it probably will."

"Maggie. We've got to find a way to stop him from going to New York."

Maggie stood up. "No, Tom. Absolutely not. I wouldn't do that to him for anything." She was surprised at her own anger. "That man has given up his dream for all these years because of Grandpa. I would not, for anything in this world, cheat him out of his second chance."

Her tone softened. "Tom, I don't want to go. Not to New York or any place else. Sometimes you just have to do things you don't want to. That's all."

"But Maggie. I might not see you again."

"Daddy says you could visit."

"He said *I* could visit?"

"Sure. Actually, he said we could have visitors. He knew I meant you. And Alfie and Gordie." She smiled. "But mainly you."

"And you'll come back, won't you? For a visit, I mean. For lots of visits?"

"Sure I will. And I might not even go. There are some details that have to be worked out. Some kind of deadline for papers to be signed. If they're not signed on time, pffht," she said, skipping one hand off the other, "the deal's off and we stay."

"When's the deadline?"

"June 30th."

"That's less than a month off."

"Three weeks."

"Does that mean you'll know for sure in three weeks whether you're going?"

"Yes."

"I'll keep my fingers crossed," Tom said softly.

"Me too. But I won't do anything to hurt his chances. In fact, I'll do everything I can to help him."

"Have you told anyone else about this?"

"No. Although I was wondering if maybe Alfie could tell."

"Nah. If Alfie knew, you'd know it. He's pretty straightforward. We ought to tell him and Gordie though, sometime. What do you think?"

"After June 30th, okay?"

"Okay."

The strawberry social ended with the same mellowness with which it had begun. Cobblers Eddy people didn't say goodbye and good night much. They just seemed to step into the shadows and not step out again, until soon the only people left were those who had volunteered to clean up.

The Baggins' vehicle was a 1922 Reo truck with benches in the back to seat 12 of the 14 Baggins offspring. The youngest two sat up front in the cab with their parents who seldom conversed on any subject. Buck had explained to Blanche years earlier that he didn't mind being with her, but he couldn't see any good reason why they had to talk.

Nevertheless, it was Buck who broke the silence. "How old is our Gloria, now?"

No response.

"I said, how old is our Gloria?"

Blanche jumped in her seat. "Me? Are you talking to me? Blanche?"

"I know who you are, woman. I said, how old is our Gloria now?"

"Oh," she said figuring quickly, "I don't know. Sixteen or seventeen, I suppose. I don't think she's eighteen yet. Maybe she is."

"I think I've found her a good man. That big kid. I liked him. Really stood up to me. Or tried to. I give him points for tryin'. What's his name?"

"Oh, I don't know. I think it's Gordie."

"What's his last name?"

"I don't know."

"Well, find out. I might want to teach him something about fixin' machines and things."

Chapter Eight

Maggie's initial opposition to moving to New York quickly gave way to her determination to see that her father received his long overdue chance to pursue his career. Whereas her mother's enthusiasm seemed to be lagging, Maggie became the move's greatest advocate. She sorted through the mail each day in search of that all important letter that had to arrive early enough on June 30th to give her father time to get it documented at the county courthouse. But the days passed, and the letter failed to arrive.

On the afternoon of June 30, she thoughtlessly let the screen door slam behind her as she hurried out the front door toward Mrs. Moss's.

"Maggie," her father said angrily. "How many times do I have to tell you not to let the screen door slam?" He was sitting on a rocking chair on the front porch with his feet on the railing.

"Oh, Daddy, I'm sorry. I thought you were out in the fields."

"What difference does it make where I am? Don't slam the screen door. It's very annoying."

"I'm sorry, Daddy."

"Just try to be more considerate, Sweetheart."

"I will, Daddy. I'm sorry." She ran for the first few yards, then began to walk. It was then she realized why her father was so irritable. It was Wednesday, June 30, the last day on which the letter could arrive. Smokey Joe had delivered the mail, and the critical letter was not there. "Poor Daddy," she said to herself.

On the way down the gravel road, Maggie saw the long, lanky figure of Smokey Joe on horseback ambling along toward her. Smokey worked at Guy Cragle's general store in the morning, then got on his horse and delivered the mail in the afternoon.

"Hey Smokes," she called to him, "did my dad get any mail?"

"Not today, Maggie. Sorry." He started to ride away.

"Wait a minute. Is there any chance he got some that's still at the store?"

"Not very likely. It's like I told your daddy jest a minute ago. I got everything that was mailed yesterday afternoon or this morning."

"But this one is from New York."

"All the way from New York? Well, that's different. Out of town mail comes in during the afternoon while I'm out, then generally gets delivered the next day. Is it important?"

"Very."

"Can't wait until tomorrow?"

"Smokey, let's get movin'."

"Now?"

"Now."

"I've got some more of today's mail to deliver, then I'll check at the store for you."

"Right now, Smokey." Maggie moved toward Smokey Joe.

"Oh, Land o' Goshen, Maggie," Smokey sighed as he put his hand down to meet Maggie's. "Come on." He spit some tobacco juice to the side. "Determined young women give me stomach cramps. Hop aboard, we'll take a look back t' the store."

Taking his hand, Maggie pulled herself up to the horse's back just behind the saddle. Off they rode at a fast trot to Cragle's store, which also housed the Cobblers Eddy post office.

There it was sitting in a small wicker basket all by itself: A thick, white envelope with her father's name neatly typed on the front and the gold embossed name of Comstock and Comstock, New York, in the upper left hand corner.

Maggie looked up at the clock on the wall: 3:20 p.m. "Smokey, how would you deliver the mail if you couldn't use your horse?" she asked.

Smokey looked down at the floor, lifted his straw hat and scratched his balding scalp. "Wall, I suppose I'd saddle up Mr. Cragle's horse an' . . . "

"Thanks, Smokey, cuz I'm gotta borrow yours right now." She grabbed the envelope, dashed out the door, unhitched Smokey's horse, swung herself into the saddle, and put the horse in a full gallop. "What's your horse's name, Smokes?" she called over her shoulder.

"Horse," Smokey Joe shouted into the cloud of dust Maggie left behind. Then he turned and shuffled back into the store where Guy Cragle was poring over a ledger book. "Ah, Mr. Cragle," he said, "I wonder if I could borrey your ol' mare for about a hour."

Maggie's father was sitting at the kitchen table writing a letter to Comstock and Comstock when Maggie burst in the door waving the letter.

"Daddy, here it is." She was out of breath.

"But where? I thought . . . "

"We got half an hour before the county courthouse closes and it takes that much time to drive there."

"C'mon, I can make it there in 25 minutes," her father said.

Twenty-seven minutes later, they were in front of the courthouse. Maggie's father jumped out of the car and ran up the courthouse steps, taking them three at a time, and disappeared inside.

Maggie slid into the driver's seat and drove the car around the block. She had never driven anything that wasn't attached to a horse before and knew nothing about the controls except how to steer. She tried pushing all three foot pedals. Two of them made ominous noises and the third slowed the car enough to enable her to round the corner. She hung on as the car whizzed around the courthouse once, then again. And again.

Soon people stopped on the street to watch her, applauding as she zoomed into view. She was too busy to wave back and her leg was getting tired from pushing on the brake. She began taking the corners faster and faster. The crowd oohed and cheered.

After 20 minutes, just as she was considering making a beeline for Cobblers Eddy without her father, he burst out of the courthouse door and danced down the steps, waving his hands in excitement and joy.

"We did it, Maggie. We by God did it," he said.

Maggie managed to wave and continued to drive around the courthouse. Her father walked to the base of the steps and waited for her to come around again.

She did. But again, she didn't stop. He started to run along side the car.

"How do you stop it, Daddy?"

"Turn off the key, you crazy adolescent," her father laughed as he caught up with her.

Once the car had stopped, he picked her up and swung her around. "We did it, Maggie. We did it. We beat the deadline by a hair, but we beat it. Yaahaahoo!"

"Does this mean we're going to be rich?"

"Maggie, that's exactly what it means. Let's go back and tell your mother."

"Do you have any money on you?"

"Yes. A little. What do you need, Honey?"

"I think while I'm here in town, I'd better pick up a little something for Smokey Joe. He's going to be very upset with me. Do you know what kind of tobacco he chews?"

Chapter Nine

Within a month, Maggie was living in a world as different from Cobblers Eddy as she could imagine. Nothing her father had said in their long discussions during the past weeks had prepared her for it.

Instead of being a land of nature where men fought for a foothold, it was a land of man made structures, paved streets, artificial light, and the constant hum of machinery in motion. It was a land of men where nature fought for a foothold.

In Cobblers Eddy, and perhaps the rest of the world, one traveled across the earth's surface to get where one wanted to go. But in New York City, one traveled vertically, up and down tall buildings, and up and down steps from the subway labyrinths that worm holed beneath the city.

Maggie felt she could never see the city properly. Everywhere she looked, there was a vertical structure blocking her view. Walking the streets, she felt like an ant inching its way through a forest of dominoes. She had to read street signs to figure out where she was.

There were endless numbers of people and they all seemed in a hurry, like Tom's father. They ignored her, and they ignored each other. People never nodded or said hello. In fact, they never looked at each other. And there were so many of them. So very, very many. It was as if a people making machine had gone berserk and spewed out nervous little people in a hurry to be elsewhere. She didn't know where. She doubted they knew themselves.

One day, as an experiment, she leaned against a florist

shop window on First Avenue and just looked into people's
faces as they came toward her on the sidewalk. No one
returned her stare. Their facial features were all so different, yet their lemming like scurryings were so alike. Maggie
felt she could walk anywhere in the center of Manhattan
and pass a continuous flow of unique faces — forever. And
never see the same one twice.

She couldn't help contrasting the pace of the city to that
of Cobblers Eddy, particularly to community events like
the strawberry social. In New York, people exploded onto
the scene — any scene. They came with the roll of drums
and the clap of thunder. While they were there, they filled
the air with bustling, frantic activity. They were all business and all energy. And when they left, the earth shook
with the deliberateness of their departures.

On Maggie's father's behalf, his partners had purchased
a five story brownstone on East 72nd Street just off First
Avenue. The great old house, with its brass door knocker
and shuttered windows, was built during the Civil War era,
had 15 rooms, and dwarfed the family furniture brought
from Cobblers Eddy. The task of furnishing the house fell
largely to Maggie and her father who shopped to their
hearts' delight at the most exclusive stores in New York.
Maggie was amazed that her father, who had been so pru-
dent in Cobblers Eddy, did not consider money an object
in New York City.

The result of their extravagant shopping was a beautiful
home from which Maggie's mother seldom ventured and to
which her father returned with decreasing regularity. The
personality of each parent seemed to become more
extreme. Her mother, who was always rather quiet,
became nearly silent. She did not feel comfortable outside
the house and didn't know what to do with herself inside.

Maggie's father, on the other hand, became more extro-
verted than ever. He was cheerful, energetic, confident and
busy in the extreme. At last he was collecting what life had
promised, but so far had denied him. To no one's surprise,
especially his business associates, he was making enor-
mous amounts of money. His talent for investments coupled with his friendly, unthreatening exuberance proved to
be a compelling combination. Maggie had to admit that her

father's rare and valuable talent had been wasted candling eggs and milking cows on a farm in Cobblers Eddy.

As time went on, Maggie was able to lure her mother out to see museums or to see an occasional play on Broadway. But her mother really didn't fit. She was still the product of an Indiana farm and felt awkward and out of place in New York. Maggie wondered if they would all have fit more naturally had her father come to New York right out of school and not spent all those years on the farm.

On a more positive note, money seemed of little importance for the first time in Maggie's young life. There was always enough. But all the money in the world couldn't keep her company. She experienced loneliness far beyond anything she had ever imagined. She missed the sounds of the farm and the smell of fresh air. In Cobbler's Eddy, there were few people spread over vast expanses of lush, rolling farm land and she knew them all. She knew none of New York's teeming millions. She missed her easy friendship with Tom, Gordie and Alfie — especially Tom.

In late summer, before school was scheduled to start, she wrote to Tom to ask him to come to New York for a visit. She wanted to send him money for the trip, but feared he might be offended. In fact, she was apprehensive about what his reaction might be to the opulence in which she lived. But she felt she had to see him.

Chapter Ten

Dear Tom,

Boy do I miss you guys. I even miss Mrs. Moss, and she never said boo to me. Heck, I miss those good old Indiana mosquitoes, the chiggers, and the poison ivy. Everything that is Indiana, I miss.

You wouldn't believe this town. There must be a zillion people here and nobody talks to anybody else. There are so many tall buildings that you can't see anything else. It's like walking in a big ditch like the one Gordie dug for his pa. The trains go underground. They really do. You have to go down steps under the sidewalk and there's a great big tunnel with trains in it that weave under the streets and stop every so often so you can get off if you want to go upstairs to the street again. In some places the trains go above the ground on these high stick like things that look like the props we use to hold up branches on the apple trees when they get heavy with apples.

Everything is paved in concrete except for a great big park right in the middle of the city.

Anyway, Daddy likes his new job — like he thought he would. We live in a funny tall narrow building called a brownstone (because it's built of brown stone, get it? It's five stories high, and we live in all five. Daddy and I bought a whole bunch of new furniture for it. (Mom likes to stay at home, so she didn't come along.) There's plenty of room if you don't mind climbing up stairs (and if you're not the one that has to carry the new furniture up the stairs).

Anyway, I want you to come up to see us. My mom says

it's all right. You and Alfie and Gordie can all come on up anytime you want, but I want you to come right now. I know it's harvest time, and I know it's a long way, but I want you to come. If you'll come to New York now, before school starts, I promise I'll come out there during my Christmas vacation.

I can't wait to hear from you. Write real soon.
Love,
Maggie

P.S. I don't care how you do it, just come. Ride Echo, hop the train, fly, drive, thumb, skate. Just get yourself here. You hear?

Chapter Eleven

During his afternoon mail run, Smokey Joe spotted Tom, Alfie and their father frantically pitching hay into a horse drawn wagon. The boys' mother, reins in hand, was standing on the load driving the horses. She was still dressed in her kitchen apron. Prompted more by the black clouds churning ominously on the south horizon than from any feelings of munificence, Smokey Joe decided to take a shortcut across the fields to deliver Maggie's letter to Tom personally.

"Y' got a letter from New York, Tom," Smokey drawled as he approached. "Or should I fetch it to the house."

"Is it from Maggie?" Tom said.

"Jes' how many folks do you know in New York?" Smokey teased as he handed Tom the letter, then eased his horse into a trot and continued on his way.

Tom opened the letter, then sat on the ground and, over his father's protests, read it quickly before picking up his pitch fork to resume work. A few moments later, the first large rain drops fell. Tom jumped into the wagon with the others as his father took over the reins, driving the excited horses in a mad dash to the barn amid high winds, thunder claps and the growing force of the rain. His father pulled the wagon into the cover of the barn only moments ahead of the storm's full fury. Tom didn't join in the laughter of relief and triumph that erupted from the rest of his family. He unhitched the horses and led them back through the rain to the lower part of the barn where he removed their harnesses, and slipped their halters over their heads. He put down a scoop of oats for them. Then, joined by Alfie, he dried them off with burlap feed bags. Alfie was talking to him about Maggie and New York and the letter, but Tom didn't hear what he was saying.

From the moment he read Maggie's letter, there was no doubt in Tom's mind that he was going to New York to see her. And he was going to begin that trip immediately.

When they finished brushing the horses, Tom and Alfie returned to the top floor of the barn and, sitting at the base of the hay mow, looked out at the rain, which by now had decreased to a steady drizzle.

"So when are we goin'?" Alfie asked.

"Before school starts, that's for sure."

"Before school? School starts in about three weeks."

"Yep. Three and a half, actually."

"The harvesting won't even be done by then."

"Maybe we could go before the harvest is over."

"Mom and Dad would never let us go before the end of harvest," Alfie said, slowly shaking his head.

They stopped talking to watch the figure of a man walk up the township road in the rain and turn down into the farm. As he got closer, they saw that it was Gordie, dressed in a tattered straw hat and a green rubber rain coat that was too small for him.

Gordie stepped into the barn. "Heard you got a letter from Maggie," he said removing his hat and shaking the water from it.

"Gordie, what are you doing here?" Tom asked. "Where'd you get the fancy raincoat?"

"I borrowed it from Eldon." he said, peeling it off. "Smokey says you got a letter from Maggie."

Tom pulled the envelope from his pants pocket and handed it to Gordie. "We're going up to see her. She invited us — all three of us."

Gordie read the letter in silence, then handed it back to Tom. "Hah!" he said. "Can't you jes' see the three of us ridin' ol' Echo on up to New York?" He looked at the other two. "So when are we leaving? Right after harvest?"

"We can't." Tom said.

"School." Alfie explained.

"So when are we leaving?" The smile was gone. Gordie

scrutinized the somber faces of the other two. "You mean we ain't goin."

"Oh we're going all right."

"When?"

"Now."

"Now? We can't go now. Our folks'd never leave us go now. And they sure as shootin' wouldn't give us a ride all the way to New York at harvest time."

Again he looked into the faces of Tom and Alfie who said nothing. "Whoa. You ain't plannin' on goin' without askin' 'em are you?"

"They'd never let us go," Tom said.

"Train," Alfie said.

"Then how are we goin' to get there?" Gordie asked, only to realize that Alfie had answered his question before he had asked it. He shot Alfie a look of mild annoyance.

The thought struck Tom and Gordie at the same time.

"We could hop in a box car," Gordie said.

"In Jim Kocher's field," Tom added, "just like we did that time with Maggie. All those trains go to New York, don't they?"

"An' it wouldn't cost us nothin'," Gordie said.

"We'd need some money."

"Not much. We could pack some sandwiches. An' Maggie's folks will feed us while we're there. So we wouldn't need much."

"But we got to tell our folks. They might let us go. Boy, wait till I tell Eldon I'm goin' to New York," Gordie said.

"We can't tell anyone. Not even your brother. If our folks find out, they'll stop us."

Gordie paced about in front of the doorway looking out into the drizzle. "I don't know," he said. "My Mom'd be terrible mad. I never done nothin' to make her terrible mad on purpose before."

"Well, neither have we. We're not trying to make our folks mad. But if we tell them, we won't be able to go," Tom said. "And I'm going."

"And my Daddy'd be powerful upset if I left before harvest is over. Powerful upset."

"We'd be back before school starts. You could still help with part of the harvest."

Gordie was shaking his head. "I can't go." he said. "I jes' can't do that to Mom 'n Dad. Can't we go later?"

"Like when? Maggie said before school starts. She's going to visit here at Christmas. If we don't go now, we'll never go. That's all there is to it."

Gordie's eyes moistened. "I can't go," he repeated. He picked up the green raincoat and shook the water off it before squeezing into it again. "When was you plannin' on leavin'?"

"Tomorrow lunchtime. When the train goes through Old Man Kocher's field, I guess." He looked over at his younger brother. "What do you think, Alfie?"

"Lunchtime tomorrow," Alfie nodded. "Come with us, Gordie."

"I can't," Gordie said placing the straw hat back on his head. "I jes' can't." He walked back into the drizzle and called back over his shoulder, "Tell Maggie I'm sorry," he said, and started up the dirt road.

After the drizzle tapered off at dawn, a gentle dry breeze from the west and patches of blue sky promised a nice afternoon. But in the morning, the ground was still too wet to work in the fields. So, like a pair of conspirators, Tom and Alfie used the respite to gather a change of clothes and to make some sandwiches. They pooled their money — including seven dollars Tom had been saving for a hunting rifle. Then, just before noon, Tom laid a note on his pillow saying, simply, "Alfie and I have gone to visit Maggie in New York. We will be back before school starts. Please do not worry. — Tom."

Carrying their clothes and food in a burlap bag, they strolled casually down the dirt road. Once out of sight of the house, they climbed over the stone wall to Jim Kocher's field and concealed themselves and their balled up food and clothes in the high grass.

Tom often sat low in the tall grass when he stalked groundhogs. He would watch the long stems sweep easily to the gentle breeze. Any out of synch movement usually signaled that a groundhog had come out of its hole and was foraging for food at the base of the tall grass. From the sway of the grass, he could distinguish between field mice and squirrels and the greater bulk of groundhogs. (Although by this method he had once inadvertently stalked a skunk, discovering his error only at the last moment.)

Even now as he and Alfie sat in silence waiting for the train, he noticed the rustle of grass some ten feet to his left and momentarily regretted not having his .22 along. Suddenly, he was startled to discover just how much grass was actually moving — all at once. He nudged Alfie whose eyes bulged. "Must be a bear." Alfie said, jumping to his feet.

"No it's jes' Gordie," came the cheerful voice of the massive teenager as he bounded out of the grass. In one hand he carried balled up clothing; in the other, a large paper bag. "Sandwiches for all of us," he said holding up the bag.

Tom was delighted. "You're coming with us? What did your folks say?"

"Didn't tell 'em. I told Eldon. He'll tell 'em later." Gordie grinned as all three sat back down in the tall grass to wait for the train.

When finally it appeared, they remained seated in the grass until the engine had passed and no one on the train could see them. Then Tom pointed to an empty wooden boxcar with its door open. They threw their food and clothing inside. As they had with Maggie a few months earlier, they ran alongside the boxcar, grabbed the edge of the door and, in a single motion, pulled themselves inside. Unlike the last time, however, there was some apprehension in this riding. All three knew they had a long ride ahead. And they knew their parents would be upset.

They sat silently as the train sped forward, leaving Cobblers Eddy behind. The only noise came from the cartons of empty soda bottles that filled half of the box car. The bottles shifted and rattled as the train picked up speed on its way east.

Tom finally spoke. "Alfie, are you okay?"

"Sure. I'm fine, just a little tired. I think I might have a cold."

"Is this what you meant the other time about there being sadness and happiness?"

"What other time?"

"The time we jumped off the train before — that day with Maggie."

Alfie thought for a minute. "No, I don't think so."

"Do you feel anything now?"

"No. Just tired."

"Whew. Why do I always feel better when you don't feel anything?"

The air was balmy — even into the evening — as the train clicked and clattered eastward. The boys began to relax, watching through the open door of the boxcar as the golden Indiana landscape flash by.

At twilight, the train slowed to a creep as it pulled into the yards at Indianapolis. Finally, with the loud squeal of brakes and some bumping sounds that reverberated down the line of cars, it stopped. The boys waited silently in the growing gloom of the railroad car a hundred miles from home. They heard the voices of workmen milling around somewhere out of their view, "No there ain't nothin' in `em to steal, but if we don't lock `em up, they're like to fill up with riffraff," someone was saying.

The boys huddled into a corner behind the soda bottle cartons. A beam of light swept across the inside of the car. There was a loud click, the sound of a sliding door and the clank of a lock. They were in total darkness.

"If either of you has a hankerin' to be scared, now's probably a good time for it," Tom whispered.

"I'd feel a whole lot better if I hadn't of heard that lock snap shut," Gordie said.

Tom groped his way in the dark to the door. He tried to look through the crack. "I think they've got a padlock on the outside," Tom said.

Gordie moaned. "Oh that's just swell."

There was a long period of silence as each of the boys dealt with his own thoughts.

Finally, the silence was broken by Alfie. "So," he said. "This is Indianapolis."

Chapter Twelve

Nine days after Maggie wrote to Tom, a single letter was slipped through the shiny brass mail slot. Her heart leaped when she saw that the return address was Cobblers Eddy. She picked it up and was about to open it when she noticed it was addressed to Tom and Alfie in care of her.

She thought about it for a moment, then opened it anyway. She recognized the precise handwriting of Tom's mother.

"Dear Tom and Alfie,

"Your father and I are real mad that you left so sudden without our OK. You could get hurt out there without our knowing about it. It would have been nice if you had let us know that you got there OK.

"Please make a telephone call to Mr. Cragle at the store. We will pay for the call. (We already worked it out with Mr. C.) Tell him if you need anything and tell him how and when you plan to come home. He will tell us what you say.

"We are mad, but we love you both and want you home.

"Love from your Mom"

It took Maggie a moment to understand what the letter meant. She showed it to her mother who called her father at work. He came home and the three of them called Guy Cragle's store and asked Smokey Joe if he would get Tom's parents to call them back immediately.

Ninety minutes later, the phone rang and the thin voice of Tom's mother was on the other end.

"Where are the boys?" she said. "They said they were off to visit Maggie. Aren't they there?"

"No," Maggie's father said. "We haven't seen them. Nor heard from them."

"Then where can they be? If they're not there, then where can they be? Tom's note said they were going to see Maggie. That was nearly a week ago. How long does it take to get to New York? Where are my boys?"

Maggie's father tried to reassure her. "Don't worry now. I'm sure the boys have just been delayed. They can take care of themselves — especially with a brute like Gordie with them." He feigned good cheer. "We'll notify the authorities here — just in case they got lost in the city. Now don't worry. That's the important thing. Those boys will be all right. I know they will."

He didn't know they would be all right. It was all bravado. And it was a bravado he would find increasingly difficult to sustain. No one even knew how the boys had intended to make the trip. Or how they were going to pay for it. No one had seen them leave.

Maggie was stunned. She had a compelling need to be doing something to find the boys, no matter how difficult; no matter how foreign to her nature.

When the first telephone conversation was over, she went directly to her room and removed the photograph of the three boys and her taken only two months earlier in Cobblers Eddy. She stuck it, frame and all, in a paper bag and headed for the front door.

"Where are you going, Maggie?" her father asked as she approached the door.

"I've just got something to do. I'll be right back," she said in an artificially high voice.

Suddenly, her father was behind her, his hand on her shoulder. "Where are you going?" he asked.

She turned around to face him. "Daddy," she said. Then she began to cry. "I have to do something. I have to do everything — everything that can possibly be done to find them."

Her father put his arms around her and she cried harder. "Where are you going now, Maggie?" he asked softly.

"To the newspapers," she whimpered. "To every newspaper in New York." She dried her eyes with a swipe of her sleeve. "I want them to run a picture of the boys. So if anyone has seen them . . . "

"Wait," her father said.

"I can't wait, Daddy. I have to do it now. This instant. I can't wait. I just can't." She began to weep again.

"Wait. Let me get my jacket. I'm coming with you. Bring all the photographs you've got. We can sort them out in the limo."

"Limo?"

"The company limo. It's waiting outside to drive me back to work. I'll ask Jesse to drive us to the newspapers instead. He knows this city like the back of his hand."

"Can you do that?"

Their first stop was the New York Times. The long, black Pierce Arrow with Jesse at the wheel swept up in front of the Times building. Maggie had the door open before the car came to a complete halt. She and her father ran into the building and found their way to the newsroom, where they were directed to the city desk. They told a red headed man in his late thirties that they would like the newspaper to run a photograph of the boys and offered to pay a reward for any information that was helpful in finding them.

The man listened without comment and without a change in facial expression. "We can't run the photograph or the plea. But we can give you a small story, if you think that might help," he said.

"Anything would help," Maggie said. "But wouldn't the chances of finding them be a lot better if people knew what they looked like?"

"I would think so," the man said. "But the Times has a very strict editorial policy that excludes that sort of thing."

"But," Maggie sputtered, "but you could help find them. They might be sick, or broke, or lost." Her eyes filled with tears.

"Zeidler," the man called out.

Another man, obviously lost in his typing a few desks away, yelled back "What?" with some annoyance at being interrupted.

"Come here."

Zeidler, a young, slightly unkempt man, approached the city desk.

"I want you to write up a brief missing persons story. These people will give you the details. See if you can work something into the story that suggests the family is offering a modest reward."

"Not modest," Maggie's father said.

"Okay, just a reward. Do what you can, will you?"

"Sure," Zeidler said.

"Don't you want the photograph at all?" Maggie asked the redheaded man.

"No ma'am. We can't use it." He paused for a moment until Zeidler was out of ear shot. "But try some of the other papers. Their policies might be different."

"Thank you," Maggie said. "We'll try them all."

The man rested his head in his hands for an instant, then rubbed his eyes as if overtaken by some great fatigue. Maggie and her father told their story to Zeidler.

The other newspapers — *The New York Sun, The Daily News, The Daily Mirror, The New York World, The New York Telegram* and *The Journal American* — were all more receptive. They all made a copy of Maggie's photograph and ran in the next day's editions. *The Journal American* asked Maggie for the photograph in which she was not cropped out and ran a story of her plight to find her missing friends.

The next day, she rode the subway to the Prospect Street Station in Brooklyn and crossed the street to take her photo and story to *The Brooklyn Eagle* on Flatbush Avenue.

For a day or two after the newspapers hit the streets, there was a flurry of responses from people who thought they had seen the boys. These leads all were checked out and proved to be blind alleys. Some of the people in Maggie's father's office volunteered to help trace the reports on their off hours.

After a week, the reports stopped. Maggie asked her father if he thought it would help to revisit the newspapers to see if they would run something again.

"No. They wouldn't run the story again, as much as they might like to. But they'd sure as shootin' run a paid advertisement, wouldn't they?"

Maggie drew up a simple ad with a photo of the three boys below the word, "MISSING." A brief copy block beneath it described the date they were last seen and offered a reward.

She took the ad to each of the major newspapers herself. Then she had the ad printed into 1,000 fliers. The ads created a brief flurry of reports, but not nearly as many as the original newspaper stories had.

She spent the next week carrying a hammer and tacks and tacking fliers to telephone poles, fences, walls and buildings. One of the first and most significant responses came from Officer Paul Roop, of the New York City Police Department, who said he understood Maggie's grief but that posting bills violated city ordinance.

She passed the remaining fliers out door to door, then asked her father if they could run another ad.

He said no.

"Then what are we going to do?" Maggie asked, her eyes starting to tear.

He looked at her lovingly, kissed her on the cheek and held her to him. "Maggie," he said, "what we are going to do now is get on with our lives."

She pulled away and looked at him. "You mean you're quitting?"

"I mean we've done it all, Maggie. There isn't anything left to do. This supposedly big, indifferent city has opened its heart to us. The newspapers, the police, the people where I work, total strangers. They all have tried to help us. If those boys were in this town — or ever had been — there'd be an army of people who would know them immediately. All we really know is that they disappeared from Cobblers Eddy, Indiana, sometime soon after they got your invitation to come to New York."

"Maybe we could advertise along the way. You know, between Cobblers Eddy and New York."

"Now, Maggie," her father said gently.

Maggie started to cry again. "I can't let them go, Daddy." She buried her face into his imported silk tie and sobbed out of control. Neither of them cared about the tie.

As the days passed, the sense of hopelessness increased. Tom's mother now sobbed openly on the phone as did

Gordie's. Maggie was beside herself with grief and worry. And she blamed herself for having asked the boys to come.

"Ride Echo, hop the train, fly, drive, thumb, skate. Just get yourself up here." Those words from her letter haunted her.

Eventually everyone but Maggie gave up. The calls from Cobblers Eddy stopped. Her parents rarely mentioned the boys. And the newspapers went on to more current affairs.

Then, finally, Maggie, her spirits crushed, gave up too. She also gave up any plans to visit Cobblers Eddy ever again. Even if her monied father paid off the mortgage, Cobblers Eddy would always be haunted for her by the three missing human beings she loved more than any others in the world.

Chapter Thirteen

The quick jerk of the train woke up the boys. It was daylight and enough light streamed through the boards and the edges of the door so they could see.

"Hey, we're movin'," Gordie said.

"And we can see," Alfie added.

"Oh, it's about time. I'm starved," said Tom. "And I wasn't about to eat last night, when I couldn't even see my food. And I only brought one jar of water."

"How 'bout some soda pop?" Gordie said.

"Yeah. Swell idea. But just a bit late, don't you think? They're all empty," Tom replied.

"Not all the way, they're not," Gordie said. "There's a little left in the bottom of each bottle and I betcha there's a hundred million bottles there."

"An' who knows what else," Alfie said.

"I'd rather thirst to death than drink that stuff," Tom said.

Alfie complained about a headache and, though he ate very little food, he drank more than his share of water. By the end of the morning, the water was depleted and the boys were forced to consider the warm, stale soda pop. All three sat on the stack, draining bottle after bottle, much as they had so often plopped cherries into their mouths while sitting in the branches of the old cherry tree at the crest of Van Horn's Hill in Cobblers Eddy.

"I wonder where we're going," Gordie said, shifting a carton behind him to get at the one beyond. "It had better be New York. If they send this car back west again, I'm gonna be powerful upset."

"They wouldn't send it east so some guy could lock the door, then send it back west," Tom said.

The boys unwrapped some of the sandwiches they had brought along. The prospect of getting some solid food in their stomachs improved their dispositions.

"I like the clacking of the tracks and the way the train sways as it moves," Gordie said. "I coulda used me some of that rock a byeing last night when I was trying to sleep. This is kinda nice."

"I like the music," said Alfie.

"You mean the sound of the wheels over the tracks and the tinkling of the soda pop cartons?" Gordie asked. "Me too."

"No, the banjo music, or whatever that is. What is it? It sounds like a banjo, but not quite."

Gordie had just bitten into a sandwich. "What music? I don't hear no music."

The two older boys looked at Alfie.

"I don't hear music either, Alfie," Tom said soberly. "Do you hear music?"

Alfie looked up from the sandwich he was holding, rewrapped it and put it back in the bag. He looked up to see the other two staring at him. "What?"

"We don't hear any music, Alfie," Tom said evenly.

"Oh," Alfie said. "I don't see how you can miss it."

"How do you feel, Alfie?"

"Not so good. I have a headache and I'm cold."

"Let me feel your forehead." He moved over to Alfie and put his hand on his brother's forehead. "I think you've got a fever."

"Oh fine." Alfie said. "We're locked in a boxcar on the way to, we hope, New York, and I get a fever. We need to get out of here. I need to get warm and get some sleep."

"I got a idea," Gordie said. "Let's make a bed out of our extra clothes. Alfie can sleep on those."

When Alfie closed his eyes for a few moments everything seemed to spin in his head. He opened them to see a familiar look on his brother's face. "You think I'm sensing something, don't you?"

"I wouldn't be surprised."

Alfie closed his eyes again. "Yeah. I do sense something. This is a very unusual train." He lay down on the floor. "And I hear music like a banjo." He closed his eyes. "And I'm not crazy about the melody. That's all there is."

Gordie leaned over to Tom, "What good does it do to have him sense things if we don't never know what it is he's sensing or what it means?"

Tom shrugged. "Sometimes we know. Let's make up a bed for him, the way you said."

Chapter Fourteen

The loss of her three best friends ravaged Maggie. For the two months after their disappearance, she practiced what she called "secret crying." She cried short spells when she was by herself and not occupied by some mental task. She almost always cried when she closed the bathroom door. She cried as she walked alone in the anonymity of New York's crowded streets. She cried as she brushed her teeth, while she got dressed, when she got into bed at night. Nevertheless, she was surprised at how well she functioned at most tasks, how she carried on normal conversation, attended to chores, arranged the day to day routines of her life.

Maggie felt she was functioning on two levels simultaneously: a public level that people were allowed to see and an inner level that was totally absorbed with the loss of Tom, Alfie and Gordie. It remained with her at all times — as she walked, as she talked, as she faded off to sleep, in her dreams, when she awoke in the night. Always. And it consumed her with sadness. She never let it go. Yet she knew they were lost for good. She knew her life must go on and would go on. And she looked forward to the day she would no longer be preoccupied by her loss.

At times, she felt they were still alive, somewhere. She felt connected to Tom, connected at the mind. If he were dead, she thought she would have felt some sort of disconnection. But she didn't.

At other times, it seemed incredible that such a trio had ever really existed. She half believed she had manufactured them from her imagination, that Cobblers Eddy never really existed, that she had been in New York all her life and had perhaps merely read a story about life in Cobblers Eddy and put herself into it. Life there had been too perfect to be real.

The rest of the world seemed able to move on, but Maggie dwelt upon her loss constantly. One cold Sunday afternoon months later, she sat at the dinner table paying no attention to her parents' conversation but instead watching absently as large snowflakes drifted like miniature parachutes past the dining room window.

"Would you like that, Maggie?" her mother asked. "Would you like it if we bought a house in Westchester County?"

She turned to see both her parents smiling at her. She smiled back weakly, but didn't reply.

"Maggie," her father said in a sing song voice. "Your mother is talking to you."

"Oh," Maggie said. "I'm sorry." But she still didn't respond to her mother's question or join the conversation.

An awkward silence prevailed for a few minutes as Maggie slowly ate her supper, apparently oblivious to the gazes her parents focused upon her.

At last, she looked up at her father. "Are they really dead, Daddy? Won't we ever see them again?"

Her father took a deep breath and returned his fork to his plate. His eyes misted over. "Yes," he said at last, "I think they are dead, but please, Maggie, don't ever ask me again."

She didn't. And, life went on.

Chapter Fifteen

Somewhere deep within Maggie's father, a powerful loco-motive steamed full bore ahead, driving him at top speed every waking hour of every day.

To his partners at Comstock, he was a prize they had plucked off a farm in Cobblers Eddy, Indiana, a hayseed with an engaging, country accent who thrived on big city turf. The more hectic the activity, the greater the pressure, the more he rose to meet the challenges. Other men's chaos was his revelry.

To his ever growing list of blue chip clients, he was a man gifted with the power and will to make them very wealthy. He had access to funds which enabled his clients to buy on margin for as little as five percent down. Within months, the value of the stocks he recommended grew so rapidly, they earned far in excess of the money borrowed to purchase them in the first place. He made his clients rich overnight and they, in turn, adored him.

To Maggie, he was a loving father who always seemed to have time for her. He also was a man with the remarkable power to make telephones ring. She could tell when he was home because the phone rang constantly. And when he stepped out the door, it stopped, as if sensing his departure.

His view of himself was modest. He made a game of adding to the number of activities he could handle at once, as a juggler adds to the objects he can keep in the air. The secret to his success as an investor was, in his view, rather simple: He persevered. He bought successful stocks —

ones that already had grown quickly. Then he watched them grow even more. He bought when stocks were high and sold when they were still higher. If a stock shot up to $10 a share, he bought and watched it go to $20, then $50, and $75. He sold only when the rate of growth began to lag. By paying off his loans from the bank, he soon became a favored client. Initially, he used the money from mortgaging the farm to buy stock on margin, first putting down $5,000 to buy $100,000 worth of stock. Soon he was routinely putting down $100,000 as leverage to buy two million dollars' worth.

He still thought of himself as a cautious country boy. He varied his portfolio to avoid getting hurt in a reversal of fortune that might strike any one company or industry. He also dealt with several banks so he would always have a source of borrowed cash.

Bankers loved him. He had everything they valued: knowledge, integrity, openness, education, wealth, and power. And he was such a kid at heart — eager, warm and not the least bit jaded by his success. They considered it an honor to supply him with the cash he needed for his own investments and for those of his clients. He was, indeed, a "Most Favored Client." Part of his popularity with bankers was his belief that it was good psychology to pay off loans regularly, then take out new ones. "Old loans make bankers nervous," he told his partners.

In addition to his ever growing personal fortune, he had two other sources of income, either of which would have supported him rather handsomely. He received a sizable commission from each investment transaction he handled himself and, in his role as a partner in Comstock, he received additional commissions for all the transactions others in the firm handled.

Only his wife's slowness to adapt to New York City marred what was otherwise a perfect transition. Although she complained very little, she was listless and seemed not to know what to do with herself. She told him once as they undressed for bed that she missed the easy pace of Cobblers Eddy. He promised to make more time for her in his schedule. But when she got out of bed the next morning, he already was in his Wall Street office working. They never talked about it again.

Maggie was all the validation his new lifestyle needed. As she slowly recovered from the loss of her three friends, she grew into a capable, confident and sophisticated young lady. Her father was certain she had gotten the best of both worlds by growing up in the health and self reliance of rural Indiana. And now she was getting the best education money and New York could provide. After graduating from the Barlow School, she entered New York University, majoring in French. He came upon her once speaking French to someone on the other end of the telephone line. He was thrilled and wondered how many teenaged girls were multilingual and could slop pigs, too. He later promised Maggie she could spend her junior year in France.

He made it a point to spend at least a part of each day with Maggie. After all, he told himself, she was the reason for it all. And he would miss her when she went to France.

In the fall of 1929, the newspapers were full of stories about panics on the stock market, but Maggie's father seemed unaffected. "It gets a little hairy sometimes, Sweetheart," he told Maggie one evening as he came in the front door, "but the thing to remember is that tomorrow things could be entirely different."

"They're calling October 29 'Black Tuesday' in the newspapers," Maggie said.

"And, for good reason. The market took a record tumble. But guess what happened on Wednesday?"

"It came back up?"

"Right. The industrial average was up 31 points, and the next day, it was up another 21. The Rockefellers jumped in and bought stocks like there was no tomorrow."

"So, what's all the fuss about?"

"Well, for one thing, the market is unstable. Quick fortunes won't be so easy to make pretty soon. Times are changing. Banks are reluctant to loan money as easily as they have in the past."

"Will we be poor?" Maggie asked.

Her father winked at her as he hung his coat in the hall closet. "Not a chance," he said, then went upstairs to his study, taking the steps two at a time.

A few days later, on a Friday, Maggie's father came home

early. His wife met him at the door. "I don't believe it," she said with a broad smile, then noticed that he was not smiling. "What's the matter?" She took his coat and hat.

"Reardon's dead. He killed himself and I just wanted to get away from the phones. The exchange is closed today. Nobody's buying. They're just talking about Reardon."

"Who's Reardon?"

"J.J. Reardon, head of County Trust."

"Would you like some coffee?"

He looked at his watch. "Sure." He followed her to the kitchen. "I've met him a couple of times. Mostly, though, I dealt with Brian Mastowe." He shook his head as he sat in a kitchen chair. "He sure didn't seem like the kind to kill himself."

"Why did he do it? Do you know?"

"No. I imagine he made some questionable deals with the bank's money. A lot of that goes on."

She put a cup and saucer before him on the table. "Just be sure you're careful," she said.

He stared off into space. "I will," he said mechanically.

A month later, he came home early again. "Sometimes, I just have to get way from that place," he told Maggie when she came home from school.

"Do you think I should go into the investment field when I get out of school?" she asked.

He laughed. "This is not the time to ask me that question," he said. "The market is not as jolly as it was a month or so ago." He thought for a moment. "No, longer ago than that." He sighed and picked up the newspaper, turned it to the financial page and sat heavily in an overstuffed chair in the front parlor.

She sat on the footstool in front of him. "Tell me about it. I want to know about the stock market. Everyone's talking about it in school. They say it's a terrible mess, that the whole country is going broke."

He put down the newspaper. "Oh, they do, do they? Well let me tell you." he said in mock seriousness.

"Really, Daddy. Tell me about it."

"Okay, Sweetie. I will." He put down the newspaper and propped his feet next to Maggie on the footstool. "First, let me assure you the whole country is not going broke. But there are some really serious problems. The stock market dips and dives, and every now and again there's an encouraging sign. But on the whole, things are getting worse. The banks loaned too much money to investors."

"Like you?"

"Well, yes, I suppose so."

"What's so bad about loaning my Daddy money to buy stock. You pay it back, don't you?"

"Of course I do. Let me explain how it works. Let's say some stock I want to buy costs $10,000. I'd come up with $500, and the banks would lend me the rest. The value of the stock would increase to $20,000. I'd sell it and pay the bank back and still have a profit of, roughly, $9,000. I'd take $5,000 of that money and ask the bank to lend me enough to buy $100,000 worth of stock. When the stock went to $200,000, I'd sell, pay the bank, and borrow again."

"So, what's the matter with that?"

"Nothing as long as the value of the stock keeps increasing."

"But it doesn't?"

"No, not always. Lately it's been decreasing. Instead of everyone benefiting, as happened when it increased, everyone is hurting. The banks, my clients, my company, the companies issuing the stock. Everybody."

Maggie thought about it for a while. "Are we hurting?"

"Well, I don't know that we're hurting yet. But you're right. Some of my personal investments have really slipped recently."

"How much?"

"Plenty."

"How much do we owe?" Maggie asked, "I mean, about."

"You are such a sweetheart, the way you say `we.'"

"How much do you think?"

"Oh Maggie, I don't know. I hate to think of it as owing. I still have the stocks I bought with the money. And, true, there is a shortfall between the value of the stocks and the amount of money I have invested in them. And the market is crazy right now. But tomorrow I could be rich again."

"How much of a shortfall? I mean the money you've gotten from the banks."

"All told?"

"Yes."

"Including my clients?"

"No, just your own," Maggie said. "How much do you think? I'm not being nosy, I just . . . "

"It's hard to be very exact about it, Maggie. The market keeps changing. But I'd say between 50 and 75."

"Between 50 and 75 what?"

"Million."

There was a moment of silence.

"Dollars?"

"Yes."

"Oh."

It was only a matter of time until they would have to give up the brownstone. Maggie's father was home more now. There was no office to go to, no finances to managed, no money to invest. He insisted that she continue going to NYU for the remainder of the semester because the tuition was already paid.

He walked a good deal. "New York is a wonderful walking town," he said by way of explanation. And he sat for hours by himself. He looked like he was brooding, but he insisted he was planning strategy. "We're not poor," he was fond of saying. "We're just broke. And you can do something about that."

Maggie came upon him one day sitting in the semi-dark of the front parlor by himself.

Thinking he hadn't seen her, she began to walk away to leave him to his solitude — something he seemed to need more in recent days.

"Maggie, come here, Sweetheart," he said.

She came in and sat on the footstool.

"All the insurance dissolved at once," he said. "I should have heeded my own advice and paid off the mortgage when I could."

"You can't?"

"No." he said unemotionally. "And the bank went belly up, calling in the mortgage in an attempt to save themselves."

"Won't the Comstocks help. You always said . . . "

"They're broke too. They have no funds."

"But . . ." Maggie said, but her father seemed not to hear. He continued to look out the window.

"You know, Mag," he said. "For the first time in my life, I feel defeated." His voice was calm, resigned. Maggie didn't like the sound of it.

"I feel like there's no way out, like things aren't ever going to get any better. Panicked. That's what it is. I don't think I've ever felt that way before. I know I haven't. I'm scared. Mortally scared. I don't have anything. I can't get anything. And, I don't have any prospects of ever getting anything again." He was silent for a few moments. "God, what I'd give to be back in Cobblers Eddy."

Maggie held him to her breast and kissed the top of his head. A couple of her tears trickled onto his hair and rolled down to his shoulder.

He sighed, exhaled heavily, and never again inhaled.

Chapter Sixteen

It was nighttime, and the train rumbled on. "Alfie, are you awake?" Tom whispered.

"I am now."

"How do you feel?"

"Better, but not that good."

Tom felt his forehead. "I think your fever is gone."

"My headache is gone, too. But I had some really weird dreams last night. I dreamed it took us so long to get to New York that . . . "

"Do you still hear the music?"

"Yep. I've heard it all the time we've been traveling and all the time I was sleeping."

"Does it mean anything to you — I mean more than it did before?"

"This is a funny train. That's what it means. It's going a longer way than we thought. But it isn't exactly going straight. No wait. That's not it. It's as if it's going a different way. You know, like sideways. Or up and down."

"Good Lord, do you think there's going to be an accident that will throw the train off the tracks?"

"Nah. I'd feel it if we were going to get hurt or killed, wouldn't I? I don't know what it means."

There was a long silence.

"You want to play 20 questions again?" Alfie asked.

"Oh, no," Tom said. I don't think I could stand another game of that. There are two things I'm never going to do again when we get out of this box car. First, I'm never going to drink another soda, even if it's fresh and cold. And the other is, I'm never going to play 20 questions again. Why didn't we bring some cards along? Or a game of some sort? Or even something to read?"

"There's not enough light to read — even in the daytime."

"But this trip is so long. If we don't get to New York — or someplace — pretty soon, I'm going to be bored right out of my mind."

The train hummed and rattled and clacked though the darkness as the brothers slept fitfully. Each envied what he thought was the sound sleep being enjoyed by the other. And both envied Gordie, who neither moved nor made a sound throughout the long, dark hours.

Gradually, light seeped through the cracks and the inside of the boxcar became visible.

Finally, Gordie awoke. "How many days have we been in this stinkin' box?" he demanded.

"Three days and three nights," Tom said. "When it's dark most of the time it's hard to keep track."

"Yeah, and we've been sleepin' at funny times," Alfie said. "Seems like we've been here most of our lives."

"It's beginning to smell like it too," Tom said.

"We've been doin' the best we can. It's hard when you can't see to go to the bathroom and you can't get rid of the stuff once you — ah, get rid of the stuff," Alfie said.

"Thank goodness for the movement of the train. I think if they'd left us sitting in a yard somewheres, the stink would have killed us," Tom said.

Outside, they could hear the high pitched shriek of the brakes.

"I spoke too soon. We're slowin' down," Tom said.

The car squealed to a stop.

"It stopped!" Alfie shouted with what the other two boys thought was excessive excitement.

"Yeah, put on your gas masks, men," Tom said.

"Not the car," Alfie said. "The music. The music stopped. The banjo music. It stopped for the first time since we started on this trip."

"For goodness sake, what does that mean?" Gordie asked. His patience had long since deserted him.

"I don't know. I don't know," Alfie said. "But it must mean something. It's the first time since we started that I haven't heard the music."

"See if you can tell where we are," Tom said trying to peek through a crack in the sliding door.

Gordie tried the other side of the boxcar. "I can't see nothin' out this side. What do you see, Tom?"

"I'm not sure. It looks like it might be another boxcar."

"Shh," Alfie said. "I hear someone outside."

Suddenly the door slid open and a wall of intense light bleached out everything within the boys' sight. They shielded their eyes with their forearms.

"Hey, turn down the lights," Gordie said. The other two laughed nervously.

A voice from somewhere within the depths of the blinding glow said, "What in damnation . . . ?"

Chapter Seventeen

Maggie hardly recognized the Comstock brothers as they emerged from a taxi in front of the funeral home. In her mind she had cast them as the villains in her ill fated move off the farm. After all, had they not intruded? Lured her father away from Cobblers Eddy? Thrust him and his family into the turmoil and isolation of New York? Had they not interfered, her father, Tom, Alfie and Gordie would still be alive.

Now here they were, looking small and forlorn in their gray striped suits, and she felt sorry for them. They stood before the casket for some moments, then turned toward Maggie and her mother, their eyes tearful and their mouths turned down. They nodded first, then said with obvious difficulty, that they would miss her father more than anyone knew.

"He was like a third brother," the taller of the brothers said. He bit his lower lip and wiped away a single tear as it rolled down his cheek.

As the two men walked slowly to seats at the rear of the room, Maggie's antipathy dissolved. "There are no villains. Just victims," she said to herself.

A half dozen of Maggie's NYU and Barlow classmates paid their respects as did a host of people who knew her father professionally. No one from Cobblers Eddy was there, of course. Maggie doubted they even knew her father had died. Both Maggie and her mother, too numb to be otherwise, were models of composure during the brief ceremony.

Within three months, Maggie got a job with a French American manufacturer of fine china as personal assistant to Roy Lamoureau, the aging president and founder. Because French was his first language, Mr. Lamoureau depended upon Maggie to rewrite his correspondence. As he gained confidence in her, he let her write the letters from scratch — in both English and French — and increasingly let her make decisions on his behalf.

She and her mother rented an apartment on West 53rd Street. While Maggie was at work, her mother stayed by herself, keeping house, listening to afternoon radio soap operas and sewing and knitting on consignment.

Maggie's work was fulfilling. As Mr. Lamoureau's health continued to fail, she accepted more and more responsibility. Inevitably, when the old man's ill health forced his retirement, the stockholders named a new president, who appointed a new executive vice president, who told Maggie her services were no longer needed.

Maggie worked a variety of jobs during the next few years, before meeting and marrying Barry Stone, a sales representative for a New York based cosmetics company. They and her mother moved to a house in Brooklyn, where Maggie gave birth to a boy she named Thomas. She never told Barry of the significance of the name, and he never asked. Maggie's conversations with him were superficial.

Barry traveled a good deal and became visibly restless when he spent more than two days at home. Typically, he came home laden with gifts for Maggie and Tommy and a knickknack for Maggie's mother. On his first night home from a trip, he was usually full of cheer as he sat with a series of scotch and waters and regaled Maggie with stories of his travels. By bedtime, he talked loudly — too loudly in Maggie's view — about how much he missed making love to her. Sometimes he followed through, but more often he fell asleep.

By the second night, after sipping scotch all day, he would fall fitfully asleep in his chair then later stagger off to bed. The next day he would get up and go to work again.

As the years went by, he came home less often, stayed for shorter periods and drank more. He seemed to have no interest in Tommy, who came to look upon him as an infrequent visitor with bad breath.

When, after an increasingly difficult five years, Maggie and Barry were divorced, Maggie felt very little emotion. She heard later that he had lost his job, but didn't know whether he had found a new one. She sued for child support, but he never paid it and she never pursued the matter. She felt more unlucky than angry at the failure of her marriage, as if she had never had a real marriage anyway.

Having her mother at home made it possible for Maggie to work to support the three of them. As the years passed, Tommy entered public schools in Brooklyn. Maggie and her mother stayed in the row house in Brooklyn as he went through grade school. Then one day as an 18 year old new high school graduate, he surprised his mother and grandmother by announcing that he had joined the Marines. He returned home after basic training and paraded proudly before his mother and grandmother in his tailored uniform, telling endless stories about his training experiences. He looked wonderful, Maggie thought, with his hard, trim body and confident air. Then one day two weeks later, he packed his duffel bag and took a cab to the Port Authority bus station. Maggie never saw him again.

He was stationed in Korea, and Maggie and her mother moved back to Manhattan so Maggie could be closer to her job with an insurance company's national headquarters.

Maggie almost received the notice of Tommy's death through her apartment intercom. At first, she refused to let the two marines enter the building. By the time they convinced her of their legitimacy, she already had guessed why they were there. She was crestfallen. Tommy's death brought back all of the old anguish of losing her three closest friends in Cobblers Eddy. She had a recurring dream that all four were together.

After that, life fell into a routine. Maggie's mother, who lived to be 94, knitted and sewed and became addicted to daytime soap operas. Maggie worked, took care of her mother, and joined the League of Women Voters. Occasionally she had male companionship, but her life's experience was that the men she loved disappeared one way or another as Tom, her father, Barry and Tommy had. And, although it was not a conscious decision, the way she protected herself from another of those painful experiences was to avoid developing rapport with men.

Chapter Eighteen

Joey Rodriguez reached for a cold Schlitz, then closed the refrigerator door with his foot. He pulled off the tab, tossed it into the trash bucket and took a long swallow, then plopped into a chair at the kitchen table.

"Ask me how work went today," he said.

"How'd work go today?" Estelle obliged.

"Don't ask me," he said shaking his head. They both laughed.

"Tough day?"

"Weird is more like it. Really weird." He took another long gulp. Estelle slid into a chair opposite him. "We got these old box cars. Been sittin' in the yard — oh, two months, maybe three. And they're locked."

"Yeah."

"An' the Flushing yard sends an order for them. So the boss tells me to make sure they're empty, see? So I goes down the row, unlocking `em and slidin' `em open. Most of `em got a lot of little shit in `em. Crates, newspapers, wood, garbage and stuff."

"Yeah."

"So I slide this one open and there's three kids inside. I couldn't believe it."

"How'd they get in?"

"I don't know," said Joey.

"How long they been in there?"

"I don't know dat either."

"Well, I mean, were they alive? I mean, how did they look?"

"They all looked fine."

"Then they couldn't have been in there long."

"Look, Estelle, they couldn't been in there — at all."

"Oh," Estelle said. "I see. And you were the only one who saw them. Right?"

"No, no, no. Loop saw them too. That is, he saw them hop out of the boxcar. C'mon — what d'ya think? I'm seein' things?"

"How would I know?"

"Anyway, I asked the kids how they got in there. They said the train slowed down and the door was open and they just ran along side and jumped in."

"How old were these kids?"

"I don't know. Teenagers. Maybe 16 or 17."

"Is that possible?"

"Is what possible?"

"That the door was open and they jumped in?"

"Never. Not in a million years. Wait a minute. I didn't tell you. They said they jumped in from a cow pasture in Indiana."

Estelle laughed. "Oh, Joey, that's a bit much,"

"Yeah, it's weird ain't it? What did I tell ya?" He drained the can of beer and looped a long overhand shot into the trash bucket.

"Two points," he said.

Chapter Nineteen

Once out of the boxcar, the boys' eyes quickly adapted to the light. They were barely noticed by a scattering of rail workers as they crossed a dozen tracks to an expansive rail yard almost entirely enclosed by a high, crumbling cement wall. Tom motioned toward an area of green that looked like it might be a way out. The three boys headed for it at a trot. They climbed a weed-obscured rusted chain link fence and crept gingerly through high weeds, trash and ashes down a steep embankment to an open drain, then up the other side to the high cement wall that encircled the rail yard. They walked along the base of the wall to an ancient metal fire escape anchored precariously to the wall.

Tom wrapped his hand around a rusted metal rod on the fire escape and tugged. "I think it will hold us," he said, looking up to the top of the wall where the fire escape led.

"It might," Gordie said.

"Maggie might be up there somewhere, you think?" he said to Alfie, who nodded.

"She sure ain't likely to be down here," Gordie said.

They climbed the rusted escape steps only to be confronted at the top by an iron fence with its slats bent outward to discourage access beyond. With some difficulty, the boys climbed over the fence and slid down a small embankment to the sidewalk. "Look at that," Alfie said, nodding toward two signs. One read "Dead End," and the other, "Warning. Trespassing forbidden for your own protection. Violators will be prosecuted."

What's that supposed to mean?" Alfie said.

"It means," Tom said, "That if you fall off the wall and kill yourself, they'll throw you in jail."

"I see." Alfie said. "A city with a heart."

"Humph," Gordie said.

The scene before them was not what they expected from the description in Maggie's letter. Instead of a bustling, energetic town, choked with people, they saw a long line of row houses stretching along a narrow asphalt street to two straight brick buildings a few blocks away. This was hardly the big city — even in the eyes of three impressionable boys who had grown up in rural Indiana.

Feeling disoriented and vulnerable, the boys stayed close together, viewing with suspicion the incredible number of automobiles parked at the curb on both sides of the narrow street. As they had in Cobblers Eddy, they walked three abreast down the middle of the street. The beep of an unexpected car behind them sent them scurrying to the safety of the sidewalk.

"That car didn't hardly make no noise," Gordie said, "and look at all of 'em. They're kinda funny lookin'. Gloria's daddy ought to see these machines." His attention quickly turned to the vapor trail left by a high flying aircraft. "Look at them clouds," he said. "The skinny ones. Didja ever?"

Tom's eyes narrowed. "There's something funny goin' on," he said, then looking at Alfie, "There is something funny, isn't there, Alfie?"

Alfie nodded, "Boy, there really is something very funny goin' on here," he said.

At the end of the street, they saw a choke of backed up traffic, and in the midst of it, three black teenage boys wiping windows and, incredibly, getting paid for it by the drivers.

Tom searched his pockets for Maggie's address. "Here it is." He squinted at a wrinkled envelope. "She lives at 409 East 72nd Street," he said. He walked through the stalled traffic to a gray rusted car with its window open. He asked the pale, balding man inside where 72nd Street was. The man pointed over his shoulder and rolled up his window. Then Tom and Alfie and Gordie walked through the waiting cars in search of another driver with his car window

open. Two of the boys who had been wiping windows inter-
cepted them.

"Get the fuck off our corner, you mother fuckin' hon-
keys," one of them said. The other snapped open a glim-
mering straight razor. "I gonna slice you meat," he said
through lips that barely moved.

The three boys almost fell over the hoods of the waiting
cars in their rush to get back to the sidewalk and around
the corner.

They stopped a man in a long black coat and asked if
this was New York and where East 72nd Street was. He
told them any one of the buses would take them to 72nd
Street, then to ask directions again to find 409 East. What
he did not tell them was that only half of the buses — those
that were headed uptown — would take them to 72nd
Street.

The boys took the first bus that came along, even though
it was going in the wrong direction and cost nearly a third
of their pooled money. As they rode, they saw a man in a
turban, grown men wearing shorts, and storefront signs
like, "The Zoo," "Adult Activity," "Swingers' Club," "VCX
Video Tape," "Live Nude Review," "Hotel Gaiety," "Calvin
Klein Jeans," "Arby's," and "Mony" — signs that made no
sense to them.

When they realized that the street numbers were getting
lower instead of higher, they got off the bus and found
themselves in Greenwich Village with all its surreality and
its crush of strange people. They saw a man in an olive
drab jacket dabbing at a gigantic painting of a little girl
who was emerging from a huge peony. From behind them
somewhere nearby came a voice they were unable to locate
saying, "Smoke? Hash?" A filthy man in rags was sleeping
on the sidewalk. They saw break dancers spinning and
rolling on the hard sidewalk surface. The crowd that
watched was at least as fascinating as the breakdancers —
including two men with identical bleached blond hair and
bleached handlebar mustaches, wearing identical pink,
bibbed overalls and no shirts who stood holding hands at
the edge of the circle.

The boys passed a group of young, tough looking white
girls; some country boys who looked a good deal like them-

selves; couples in their 20s and 30s; several beautiful, young, scantily dressed, naive looking girls in their early teens; several whorish looking older women; and college kids. With the exception of the derelicts, who were scattered here and there on the streets, they saw few people of middle age or older.

They paused very briefly to join passersby who had stopped to look in the window of a store called "My Sweet Dreams," expecting to see a performance of some sort. A sign in the window said, "August is Bondage Month." The shop was half a flight down from the sidewalk so one could see the whole inside of the shop with men and women customers examining the various leather bondage straps, shackles, whips, soft ropes, trusses and exotic clothing. But what caught the boys' attention were two inflatable life sized naked female dolls wearing bikini pants that were open at the crotch. The dolls had their arms handcuffed behind them and stainless steel clips fastened to their nipples. The clips were joined by a stainless steel chain, the clear implication being that a naked woman, her hands trussed behind her, could be led around by the chain fastened to the clips on her nipples.

"That's awful," Alfie shouted loudly as he looked wide eyed into the window. "Why do they let them show that awful stuff?" He covered his face. "Let's get out of here. This is a crazy town. Let's go home."

As they walked, they heard, close to their ears, "Smoke? Hash?" They were unable to tell who said it.

Alfie saw a young girl carrying a pie pan from which she was shoving some sort of salad into her mouth with a white plastic fork. He tugged on her sleeve. "Excuse me, where did you get that?" he asked.

She laughed self consciously at being caught with her mouth full. "Ummh," she said pointing over her shoulder with the plastic fork. "Back `ere. Delicatessen." She laughed again, poked another forkful of food in her mouth and went on her way.

Alfie squinted at Tom. "What did she say?"

"Back there at the delicate something."

The boys headed back in the direction she had pointed and found themselves in front of what looked like Guy

Cragle's store. A man wearing sunglasses came out the door carrying a paper bag.

"Is this a grocery store?" Alfie asked.

Even through the dark glasses, Alfie could tell the man was startled by the question. "Yeah," the man said. "It's a delicatessen." He walked on.

All three boys looked at each other. "Del-a-ca-tess-en," they said in unison and walked inside.

After examining the choices, and the prices, they counted their money and decided to buy a loaf of Wonder bread and three one-pint cartons of white milk.

They walked out of the store, each eating a slice of plain, white bread. "I love food," Alfie said.

When they got outside, Tom said. "Okay. Here's my plan: See those yellow cars with the `taxi' signs on their roofs? I've been watching them. People pay them to take them places. We call one over and tell him Maggie's exact address."

"But we don't have enough money left, do we?" Alfie said.

"I'm getting to that," Tom said. "We tell the driver to head for Maggie's house and to keep on going until we run out of money, then to let us out. We'll walk the rest of the way."

Alfie whistled. "Wow, Tom. That could mean a lot of walkin'."

"So what? I figure we'll get to her house some time in the morning. That's lots better than arriving in the middle of the night."

Gordie raised his eyebrows and reached into his pocket. "That sounds pretty good. I still got me a dollar bill and then some." He handed the money to Tom.

Alfie reached in and pulled out a small handful of change, which he handed to his older brother.

"And, I got some change and a dollar," Tom said.

The boys finished off their cartons of milk and dutifully placed the empty cartons in the trash baskets along the curb. Then Gordie folded up the bread wrapper and put it back in the paper bag.

"Are you ready?" Tom said to Gordie.

"Yep. I'm ready." Gordie said. "Are you ready, Alfie?"

"I'm ready." Alfie said.

"Well," Tom said, hitching his pants up. "Then here we

go."

He walked to the curb and put his hand up. People began to look at him.

"Shouldn't you wait until there's taxi car?" Alfie asked.

"Right, I guess I better," he said, then shouted, "hey, taxi," as one appeared.

The taxi pulled to the curb, and Tom showed the driver, a Middle Easterner in his mid-30s, the return address on Maggie's letter. "Can you take us to this address? 402 East 72nd Street?"

The driver smiled agreeably. "I take you," he said.

"Okay, but we only want to go part way — as far as three dollars will take us. Okay?"

"You got money?" the driver said.

"Yes, three dollars," Tom said.

"I take you," the driver said. "Get in, I take you." He smiled as he reached back to open the rear door for them.

During the next ten minutes, the three boys from Cobblers Eddy got a quick look at the magic of New York City at night. The lights fascinated them. Although it was not exactly like daylight, it was not like any night time they had known, either. They wouldn't mind walking through the night, they thought, if it was going to look like this.

Suddenly the taxi stopped. "That is 409 East 72nd across the street. So you want me to pull up in front?"

"But," Tom stuttered. "I I thought you were going to tell us when we used up three dollars."

The driver smiled. "No, please," he said, pointing to the meter, "is six dollar and 20 cent."

"But we only have a little over three dollars," Tom said.

The driver stopped smiling, but remained polite. "Is six dollar and 20 cent. It say so on the meter."

Gordie spoke lowly to Tom. "Maybe we can borrow the rest from Maggie."

Tom shrugged. "I guess we'll have to." He handed the driver all the change he had collected plus his own dollar bill.

"We'll have to get the rest from our friend," Tom said.

The driver looked at the change and got out of the taxi. He kept examining the change.

"This is old money," he said, examining the coins. "Very

old."

Tom was puzzled. Why did the age of the money matter? "We'll get the rest from our friend," he said. The three boys got out of the taxi and walked over to the driver, who kept examining the handful of coins they had handed him.

Just then, a police cruiser pulled up. A policewoman, who was sitting in the passenger side, leaned out the window and said, "You got a problem, Cabbie?"

The driver looked up at her. "Yes, I have a little problem, I think," he said.

The red dome light went on and both the policewoman and her partner, a portly man with a thin, black mustache, got out of the car. "Look at these coins, officers," the driver said. "They're all old — 1920s or before. Looks like they from old coin collection. Also, meter say boys still owe three dollar more."

"Where'd you get the coins from?" the policeman asked the boys.

The three boys were panicked. No one answered.

The lack of response angered the policeman. His voice took on an edge. "Did you steal them, boys? Did you take somebody's valuable coin collection that they spent years collecting and just spend it like it was just plain ordinary money?"

"We're not crooks," Gordie said. "We never stole nothin'. Not never. If you don't believe us, ask Maggie."

"Who is Maggie?" the officer asked.

"She's our friend," Alfie said.

"Yeah," Gordie said. "We come all the way from Cobblers Eddy, Indiana to see her."

Tom nodded toward a worn, recently painted, brownstone positioned between two apartment buildings across the street. "She lives right there, across the street, at 409, Officer," he said.

The police officers huddled with the taxi driver. "What do you say? If the girl pays for the cab fare, will you drop your complaint?"

The cab driver shrugged his shoulders. "Sure. I don't care."

"There's still the old coins," the policewoman said.

"Bah," her partner said. "There's no law against havin'

old coins."

"But they sure musta stole them from somebody."

"Yeah, but who? It's only a couple of bucks, and nobody's complainin'. So what are we gonna do? Let's just scare the bejesus out of 'em and let `em go."

She nodded, "What ever you say, Ace."

The policeman turned back to the boys. "Okay. What's the girl's name?"

Tom handed him the letter. "It's right here," he said pointing to the name neatly written in the upper left hand corner of the envelope.

The policeman yanked the letter out of his hand. "What are you guys tryin' to pull? A two cent stamp?" He showed it to the woman policeman and pointed to the postmark. "Does that say what I think it says?

She looked at it. "August 17, 1926," she said.

"It's postmarked in 1926," he said to Tom.

"Right." Tom said.

"Can you explain that?" the policeman said.

"Well," Tom said, looking at the envelope. "I don't know. I thought they were all dated."

"1926?"

"Yeah. I mean yes, Sir."

The policeman studied Tom for a moment. "What year do you think this is?" he asked.

"1926, Sir," Tom said.

The policeman rubbed his jaw, then turned his gaze to Gordie. "And, what year do you think this is?" he said.

"It's 1926," Gordie said.

He looked at Alfie who was visibly shaken. "And you?" he said.

"I — I don't know," Alfie said.

The policeman raised his eyebrows. "You're the closest one yet," he said. "Okay, all three of you, put your hands on the squad car, feet apart." He searched them quickly, then told Gordie to put one hand behind his back. When Gordie did, the policeman snapped on one handcuff. "Okay, the other hand," he said and snapped on the other. The woman handcuffed Tom and Alfie together at the wrists.

Within a moment, another squad car pulled up and two

burly male policemen got out. "We'll take the big one," the black policeman said, pulling Gordie by the material on his shirt sleeve.

Alfie watched wide eyed as he and Tom were led into the back seat of the first squad car. "This is not real. It's like a dream," he said.

Just then an ambulance sped up First Avenue, its siren blaring. When it got to 72nd Street, the siren changed tone, sounding "weep weep weep weep weep." Amid the din, the black policeman pushed Gordie's head down to make him fit into the back seat of the second squad car. "This is no dream," Gordie screamed in panic. "It's a nightmare." The squad car door slammed on his final word, and both cars zoomed off, their sirens adding a frantic counterpoint to the ambulance's.

Chapter Twenty

At 4:22 p.m., Margaret Stone heard a muffled giggle from one of the young secretaries and looked up just in time to catch a glimpse of someone carrying a huge, ornate cake into the conference room. In spite of her orders, they were indeed going through with the retirement party. Margaret was not pleased.

She put down her pen and went out into the hall. It was too late to escape. Patronizing smiles blocked her exit in every direction.

She scowled into the crowd of well wishers and put her hand up. "Ho no you don't," she said.

"We have a little surprise for you," came the sing-song voice of Madge Patterson, the claims supervisor. "In the conference room."

Margaret stood silently for a moment, her mind racing. "You folks go ahead. I'll join you in a bit. I have some last minute work to catch up with."

"Mr. Mann's orders," someone said. "He said we should escort you to the conference room."

"Yeah, no excuses," someone else added, among the laughter and applause.

"Where is Mr. Mann?" someone asked. "We're ready to start as soon as Mr. Mann gets here."

Margaret walked grudgingly through the midst of her coworkers into the conference room and to the scene she had witnessed so often over the years. Once it had even been the setting for a going away party for a temporary secretary who had been there less than two weeks.

Mr. Mann had been late for that one too.

A high gloss, black conference table dominated the room, with 10 matching chairs and a long, narrow buffet table. Margaret hated the room because it was too small. The furniture had been bought for an earlier, larger conference room.

So, for the past decade, people had entered the conference room in single file, with the first person taking the chair in the farthest corner and giving an unspoken promise that they would not be the first to leave.

Today, Margaret had the dubious distinction of being the first one in the room. She sat, trapped, at the end of the table as others sat around and made small talk. A cake, soft drinks, coffee, and several bottles of wine sat in the middle of the table. Nobody touched anything.

"Ah, does Mr. Mann know we're ready?" asked Arnold Garnett.

"I've got an idea," Margaret said. "In honor of my faithful years of service, let's start without him."

Everybody laughed, but nobody moved toward the food.

"I heard that, Margaret," came the voice of Mr. Mann followed soon by his round, smiling face around the corner of the door jam.

Everyone laughed again, and the phone rang. Millie answered it. "It's for you, Mr. Mann," she said.

"I'll take it in my office. I'll be right back." He started to leave, then turned back and pointed a finger at Margaret playfully. "Now you behave yourself, Margaret," he grinned.

Everyone laughed, their hands folded on their laps. Millie rose and lit the four candles on the table.

Margaret stood up and put her hand out to the young girl sitting next to the door. "Give me the knife," she said sternly.

The girl handed her the knife. Everyone laughed again.

"How many people are there here?" she said.

"Counting Mr. Mann?" someone said.

"No," she said. "Not counting Mr. Mann. Just counting those who actually are here."

Laughter.

When she cut into the cake, the laughter stopped.

"Margaret," Arnold said. "You can't do that. We have to wait for Mr. Mann. After all, he . . . "

"Arnold," Margaret said with emphasis. "Open the wine."

"But Margaret."

"Do you open the wine, or do I open the wine?"

Arnold looked at her for a moment, then smiled. "I'll open it. You'd break off the neck of the bottle against the edge of the table and pour the wine through the broken glass."

"You're right, Arnold, I would. Pour the wine."

Everyone laughed again.

A few minutes later, Mr. Mann came in. He was mildly surprised that people had started without him, but had the poise to say he was glad they hadn't waited. He sat, the focus of attention, telling about his younger years as a novice leader of the masses. Margaret found the stories self aggrandizing and unspeakably boring.

Soon one of the young secretaries excused herself, explaining that she had to meet her husband. Another had to catch a bus, and a third had company coming. They all said their goodbyes to Margaret and asked her to stop in or to come to the company picnic in the fall or to give them a call sometime. Soon the only ones remaining were Mr. Mann and those who were not very deft at bowing out.

Margaret said her own goodbyes, explaining that she still had some finishing up work to do before she could leave. Everyone on one side of the table went out single file to let her out. Millie began to clear off the table.

A few minutes later, Millie came into Margaret's office. "There," she said, flopping a New York tabloid on Margaret's desk. "I told you I had heard of Cobblers Eddy. Read the caption under the photo. These kids claim to be from Cobblers Eddy, but no one from Cobblers Eddy has ever heard of them."

Margaret felt a numbness in her hands, feet and in the roof of her mouth as she very nearly fainted dead away. Not because of the caption, but because the three boys in the photo were dead ringers for Tom, Alfie and Gordie — exactly as they looked the last time she saw them — nearly six decades ago. She turned pale and stumbled back into her chair.

"Oh my goodness," Millie said. "Are you all right, Margaret? What's the matter. Are you okay?"

Margaret waved her hand. "I'm okay." She stared at the photo of three boys sitting on a bench.

"What is it?" Mildred said. "What's wrong?"

"Those boys," Margaret said softly. "They look . . . they look like . . . They're dead ringers for. Tom, Alfie and Gordie."

"Who?"

"Three boys I grew up with. I can hardly believe it." She looked at the paper again. "That's just incredible. Just incredible. I've got to get in touch with them." She shook her head again. "They look so much like . . . "

Millie looked at the paper again. "Could they be relatives of some people you knew?"

"They'd have to be. I haven't been back in nearly 60 years." She was still shaken as she looked at the photograph again and read the caption. It said:

COBBLERS WHAT? — Three teenagers find they can't go home again because no one at "home" has ever heard of them. The trio said they made the trip to the Big Apple in a box car from tiny Cobblers Eddy, Indiana, (pop. 135).

"Millie, will you do me a big favor? Will you make some phone calls to help me find where the boys are now? The bench they're sitting on looks like it might be in the city government somewhere — the police station, social services — someplace like that. I think I ought to talk to them."

"Sure Margaret. You may be able to help them. I'll make some calls right now if you'd like." She started to leave.

"And, Millie. This is just between you and me, okay?"

"Sure, Margaret. I understand. I'll call you as soon as I find them." She walked into the hall, then stopped and looked back. "I was right, wasn't I. I had heard of Cobblers Eddy, hadn't I?"

Margaret raised her eyebrows. "You had indeed, Millie."

Satisfied, Millie left.

Margaret looked at the paper again. "Incredible," she said out loud. "I wonder if this is some kind of mistake — that they used an old photo or something — maybe a file picture from long ago. Nah. Maybe it's just my eyes. Or my imagination. Whew! This isn't really happening."

She swiveled her chair toward the window and looked out at the borough of Manhattan sprawled for miles before her. It was a scene she had viewed countless times before but this time was different. This time her focus was on the mass of humanity the city held in its choked streets, busy sidewalks and tall buildings. "Could they be out there after all these years?" she wondered aloud. A chill ran down her spine. She knew full well such a thing was not possible.

Chapter Twenty-One

"So how do you like retirement so far?" It was Millie calling Margaret at home mid-morning the next day.

"So far, it smells — like day old fish," The old woman said, drawing a howl of laughter from the other end of the line.

"I found the boys. They're guests of the city."

"They're in jail?"

"Well, not exactly. They're at the New York City Hospital psychiatric clinic where they're apparently making a big hit. The guy I talked to on the phone said they were about the nicest crazy kids they'd ever had in there."

"That's a bit severe, don't you think?"

"I think he was trying to be funny. The police turned them over to the welfare department, which turned them over to the clinic, which wanted to `study' them."

"Study them?"

"That's what I said. The guy said the prospect of interviewing and examining three seemingly sincere and honest young men who shared the same illusion was the chance of a lifetime."

"Yeah, the chance of a lifetime for him. But what about the boys?"

"Actually, it's not a bad deal for them either. They get food and a place to stay for a couple of days, then the clinic will put them up at a youth hostel for a couple of months till they get settled. Till they get jobs, I guess that means."

"Yeah. And, they probably get free medical." Margaret said. "So how do I get to see them?"

"They'll be at the clinic for another day, then at the hostel. You can visit them there."

"Do you have the address?"

"No, but they're in the book. It's the one on York Avenue, at about 58th Street. And, Margaret, I got the impression that they're really taking these kids under their wings. I don't think they're just going to dump them at the hostel and forget them. I think they're going to look after them. And, I think the welfare people are still involved, too."

It was a case worker from the welfare department who, three days later, arranged for Margaret to meet the boys. He volunteered to personally deliver them to Margaret at her apartment, provided she would return them, in person, to the youth hostel.

In preparation for their visit, she got out all the old photographs of her family and friends from Cobblers Eddy — including copies of those she had taken to the newspapers more than half a century earlier. She was struck once again by the uncanny resemblance. She had by now half convinced herself that these were indeed the same boys, catapulted through time and space somehow to meet her in New York City in 1984. This moment as she looked over old photographs in the privacy of her own bedroom seemed to Margaret quintessentially personal. She looked over her shoulder to be sure she wasn't being observed. Suddenly, she caught a glimpse of herself in the hall mirror, a pathetic, lonely old woman scavenging through musty cardboard boxes in search of faded photographs of three boys who had been dead since her childhood. She got scared and moaned in despair like someone's pet dog left for too long in an empty apartment. The sound of her moan reverberated throughout the emptiness and added to her misery.

"I am crazy," she said to herself. "What part is real and what part did I imagine?" Tears filled her eyes and streamed down her wrinkled cheeks until she could no longer see the old photographs. "Oh dear," she said out loud. "I must put these away and get hold of myself." She stuffed the photographs in the box and pushed it with her foot into the hall closet. She looked at herself in the mirror, and dabbed her eyes with a handkerchief. "Oh dear, oh dear," she said, still looking into the mirror. "Those poor boys. It's not enough that they're away from home, they almost fell into the clutches of a crazy old woman who thought they were her long lost childhood friends. Whew. I've got to be careful."

When the doorbell rang, her heart pounded as she tried to picture what might be waiting for her on the other side of the door. In spite of the lecture she had just given herself, she half expected to see three boys in sepia tone like one of the old photos.

She opened the door and was met by a smiling middle aged man in a tweed jacket and tie. She looked at him blankly for a moment, then caught her breath quickly as she looked beyond him. There, in full color and three dimensions, were the three shy country boys of her youth.

The man in the tweed jacket was saying something that Margaret was not listening to when Alfie darted past the others, threw his arms around Margaret, and murmured something into the folds of her sweater.

"What did he say?" Tom asked rather coldly. "Did I hear what I thought I heard? What did you say, Alfie?" Then, looking back at Gordie, "Did you hear what he said?"

"No," Gordie said.

Alfie kept hugging. The tweed jacket spoke again. "These are the three boys you asked about, Ma'am. Just be sure they don't get lost. If you have any trouble getting them back to the hostel, give me a call. Don't just send them out on their own. We may never find them again. You wouldn't believe how little they know about getting around in the city." He tipped his hat and closed the door behind him without waiting for a response from Margaret.

"I'm Tom," Tom said, extending his hand which Margaret shook. "And this one clinging to you is my little brother, Alfie. And this here is Gordie."

"Pleased to meet cha," Gordie said awkwardly.

Alfie pulled away and stood close to Margaret, glaring at the other two.

"What did you just say?" Tom asked.

Alfie began to cry and hugged Margaret again as the old woman stood dumbfounded.

"I don't know what's the matter with him." Tom started to say. Then he looked at Margaret's face and saw tears welling up.

Alfie pulled away and through angry sobs blurted out: "I said, `I love you Maggie.' You dopes, this is Maggie."

"Holy Smokes," Tom said, sinking to one arm of the sofa. "I heard you say something about Maggie, but I never thought." He curled his bottom lip under his upper teeth and took a couple of sharp breaths then began to weep. "Maggie. What happened to us? What happened to you? You're an old lady, Maggie. You're an old lady, and I'm only 17."

"This here is Maggie?" Gordie asked good naturedly. "Gee, are you really, Ma'am?" He looked at her closely. "Nah. That can't be." He picked up her bony, freckled hand and inspected it. For a moment, he couldn't talk. He continued to look at her hand rather than at the woman it belonged to. And he avoided eye contact with the other boys. "That's not fair." He kissed her hand and tears streamed down his tanned cheeks. "I'm telling you, Maggie, it just. Ain't. Fair." Great heaving sobs followed that shook every inch of Gordie's considerable bulk.

The room, which a few moments before had been so silent, now echoed with the sounds of sobbing.

Alfie continued to sob softly into the sweater of the elderly woman who was herself fighting back tears. Tom sat hunched on the arm of Margaret's sofa weeping into the crook of his arm. And standing nearby, Gordie shook with loud, deep sobs he could not control.

Deep inside her head, Margaret backed up to a wall past which incredulity could push her no further. She began to laugh. This was wonderful and absurd at the same time. Until now she had stood frozen while Alfie hugged her. Now she hugged him back and laughed harder. There was joy in her laughter but there also was defiance. After the emotional roller coaster she had ridden during the past week — a ride ending in the dumping of three resurrected boys at her doorstep — she thought there was nothing life could deal her now that she could not endure. And that sense of invincibility made her certain she could handle this — and probably any other situation that came along.

She heard the shrillness of her own voice rise above the din. "Where in hell have you guys been?" she shouted, shocking the boys as much with her language as her volume.

They looked at her dumbly. "We took the train," Tom said soberly.

"That was 58 years ago." Margaret trumpeted, a smirk on her face that made the boys a little uneasy. "What kind of a train did you take?"

Tom shrugged. "You know. That train. The one that goes through Kocher's field."

"Yeah, the slow train," Gordie said. He ducked his head sheepishly as the others laughed, their faces still streaked with tears.

"Well, you got here. I suppose that's the important thing." She looked at the boys and they at her. "But 58 years." She said smiling calmly now. "Couldn't you have hurried things up and made it in, say, 25?" The smile left her face. "You guys haven't changed in all that time. This is the single most incredible moment of my life. You are exactly the same. I remember every pore on your faces." She glanced at the buffet mirror. "But I've changed."

"Not that much," said Alfie. "How old are you?"

"Seventy-four."

"Whoa! That's old," Gordie said.

"What year were you born?" Margaret asked.

"Aught nine. Me and Tom both were born in aught nine." "You're 75."

"No. We're 17. Both of us."

"We've got to talk about this," the old woman said. "No, first we've got to have some coffee."

Alfie started to cry again. Then Tom. Gordie bit his lower lip to hold back the sobs.

"No," Margaret said, "First we gotta cry, then we gotta have coffee. Maybe we can cry while the water is heating up, then . . . is instant okay?"

She got three blank stares. "What am I saying? Do we drink coffee?" she asked.

"No, only grown ups drink coffee," Alfie said. "But we drink tea if you've got any. With milk and sugar."

"Would you rather have a glass of wine . . . or a highball? Sorry, I don't have any beer." She thought for a moment. "Are you guys old enough to drink?"

"I think I'll be 74 on my next birthday," Alfie said. "Is that old enough?"

"You'll only be 72, you rascal. I think we'll have tea, anyway. Come on out into the kitchen," Margaret said, leading the way. "The man said to keep a close eye on you guys, and that's what I'm planning to do."

They followed her into the kitchen, where she filled a tea kettle with water and put it on the stove. She pushed a button and the heat coil began to glow.

Gordie watched in awe. "Is that stove 'lectric or somethin'?" he asked.

"No doubt about it," Margaret said. "You push these buttons, depending on how hot you want these coils to get, then they turn red when they get hot."

"Mr. Cragle has one like that. Only his has a big like spring that winds around and you turn a knob. And you have to plug it in."

"Yes, I think I remember it." Margaret said. "Caught fire or something, didn't it?"

"Blew up." Gordie looked at the stove again. "Wasn't as nice as yours. He got it fixed, and now it's working fine."

For a fleeting moment, Margaret was tempted to remind Gordie that it was 1984 in Cobblers Eddy too, but thought better of it.

The boys were fascinated by the shape of the tea kettle, by the fact that it whistled, by the stainless steel sink, the fluorescent lights in the kitchen, the electrical outlets, the wall to wall carpeting, the fact that the windows of Margaret's high rise didn't open, by her cassette stereo, her color television, and by the quietness of her flush toilet. A machine that actually washed and dried dishes was, to them, beyond the pale. And they kept covering their eyes when they came close to a window because the view down to the street made them nervous.

When the tea was ready, Tom and Alfie joined Margaret at the kitchen table while Gordie stood a few feet away opening and closing the venetian blinds.

"What was it like?" Margaret asked. "Your trip. How long did it take? When did you realize you had, you know, traveled here and now?"

"We didn't know," Tom said. "Someone locked us in and

it was dark and stinky for a couple of days. I was surprised when I found out where we were."

"I wasn't," Alfie said. "It was just like I pictured it."

"Well, I was scared. I can tell you that, boy. And hungry. We coulda starved to death in that box car thing if nobody'd let us out."

"Do you know what I don't understand?" Margaret said. "I don't understand how it was all possible — how you traveled in time to get here. To me, that's the real mystery. I know you got locked in a boxcar way back then and when you came out, it was now. But why? Does that happen to everyone who gets locked in a boxcar? Would it happen to you again? I don't think so."

"I been thinkin' about that," Tom said. "But who would do that to us? Who could do it — and why?"

"I did a lot of thinkin' about it at first," Alfie said, "but I don't any more."

"But nobody even knowed we was comin'," Gordie said. "We even hid from the people on the train. Nobody saw us."

"Well, you certainly have done something highly unusual," Margaret said, "but it just doesn't make sense. I suppose that's why it bothers me so." Margaret thought for a moment. "I met a man once who told me not to worry about things I couldn't figure out. He said I knew so few of the things that were knowable that one more or less didn't add up to much. And I'm not even sure this one is knowable."

Margaret put a deep pan of water on the stove and measured a plentiful supply of spaghetti while the boys tried to figure how to make the water come out of the shower nozzle. Somehow, they finished up showering just as she finished making a quick salad. They sat at the table, each with his moist hair brushed neatly to the side of a somewhat tentative part.

Conversation at the table was easy and unstrained. The four exchanged stories with Margaret doing most of the talking. The boys were sorry to hear that they had caused such heartbreak when they disappeared. Margaret was reluctant to mention the deaths of her parents or her son because she thought it would be difficult for the boys to hear too much too soon. They didn't seem to fully realize that it was 1984 in Cobblers Eddy just as it was in New York City. They understood, intellectually, that it was 1984 all over the world, but somewhere inside their heads they still pictured the Cobblers Eddy of 1926. No one mentioned that their parents, for instance, probably had been dead for years. When the boys spoke of Cobblers Eddy, they did so in the present tense. It was like finding a radio from one's childhood and being surprised that it no longer broadcasts the old programs, but instead plays rock music and McDonald's commercials.

That night, as the boys sprawled out on the living room floor, Margaret lay awake in her room. She worried about the immediate future and fretted about how she hated being old when she need so to be young and energetic. She thought of all the catching up the boys would have to do to make it in the modern world. She also had a vague dread of falling asleep for fear she would wake the next day only to find she had imagined this whole incredible reunion. She could faintly hear the boys — mostly Gordie and Tom — talking softly in the other room. As she was drifting off, she thought she heard someone say, "We found Maggie and lost everybody else."

Early the next day, Margaret took the boys back to the youth hostel and sat in a waiting taxi while they went inside to get their few possessions. Without asking anyone's official permission, she moved them in with her. Her plan was to take them back to Cobblers Eddy when she went back herself — probably in a few weeks.

In spite of the tremendous confusion that stirred within the boys, they were delighted to be with Margaret. For the first three days, when they felt most disoriented, they didn't let her out of their sight. Although she was changed by time and now called herself Margaret, the elderly woman remained their only link with their own world and, quite possibly, their only link with their sanities. Of the seven million people in New York City, Margaret Stone was the only person who believed they had actually traveled through time in a boxcar.

Margaret lectured the boys inordinately about the perils of modern life in the big city. They listened attentively, but there was a sadness in their countenance that broke her heart. She caught herself being comforted by thoughts of the trip back to Cobblers Eddy. "Everything will be fine for them back in their own surroundings," she would say to herself, then would add, "no it won't. Cobblers Eddy will be a caricature of itself. It'll be a strange combination of yesterday and today with all of the people they loved gone — gone and replaced with strangers who won't have any place for three teenaged boys who say strange things about time travel in a boxcar."

If these three precious boys were going to succeed anywhere in 1984, there was a great deal they had to learn. She told them about credit cards, World War II, income taxes, herpes, plastic Christmas trees, punk rock, women's lib, computers, pay toilets, hookers, pimps, Clark Gable, Marilyn Monroe, Walt Disney, miniature golf, go-go dancers, *Playboy Magazine,* alphabet soup, the pill, the Beatles and VW Beetles, the space program, President Kennedy and the second President Roosevelt, Vietnam veterans, the Korean War, Ayatollah Khomeini, nuclear fission, pizza, and the stock market crash.

The boys listened and learned.

Chapter Twenty-Two

Working with the boys was clearly the focus of Margaret's post retirement life. She was a field marshal in an all out offensive to assure their survival in 1984. She wanted them to be as tough as the past 58 years had made her. But she wanted them to do it in a matter of months.

New York City, where the boys knew only her, was an excellent proving ground. When they got to Cobblers Eddy, they would know other people — people altered by age as she was. It was hard to imagine how the residents of present day Cobblers Eddy would be — whether they would believe the boys or not. But, in Margaret's view, the boys had to survive and succeed. And Margaret saw it as her foremost mission to make sure they did.

Her instruction was highly structured and deliberate. She taught the boys to bargain at the market place and to argue with taxi drivers about the best routes across town. She taught them to give directions to tourists and to ride every subway and most of the buses to the end of the line.

She took them through department stores, grocery stores, and delicatessens to learn relative values. Then she sent out each one alone to do the shopping. She taught them to read bus, train, and airline timetables, to use various directories at the library, and how to quickly disengage from anyone trying to con them.

Soon the boys started looking for challenges. They would find a street corner con man working a shell game, for instance, just for an opportunity to bait him.

She was proud of them for having learned so quickly and so willingly and she was delighted with the camaraderie that had developed between the boys and her. It was a far cry from the camaraderie they had shared in her youth in Cobblers Eddy, but it nevertheless made them close.

She inherited three country bumpkins from 1926 and turned them into three 1984 New York City sophisticates. And, through this arduous metamorphosis, none of the three lost any of his sweetness and warmth. Margaret was exceedingly well pleased.

As the weeks went on, Margaret was aware of some changes in herself as well. Reality became almost a matter of viewpoint. It was her secret opinion, for instance, that she had brought about the boys' reappearance after more than half a century by the magnitude of her love for them and by her unwillingness to let them go. She had profoundly wished for their safety and well being over the course of most of her life. Now that, by some miracle, they were here, she felt she should have prepared a better world for them to re-emerge into. They, on the other hand, unwittingly fueled her feelings of guilt and insecurity by their adverse reactions to New York City in 1984.

One day as they watched the local news, Tom said, more in an attempt to be clever than anything else, that New York City was full of "din, dirt, and danger."

Margaret said nothing at first. But when the news was over, she defended herself against the guilt she had felt so long and so unreasonably: "One thing I want you guys *not* to do," she said, "is hold me personally responsible for the way the world turned out over the past half century or so. I really didn't have that much to do with it." She paused between sentences. "I just wasn't able to exert that much influence. I wanted things to be lovely and sweet, the streets to be clean. I didn't want muggers, or noise, or pollution. Or poor people, or anger, or pain. I wanted everyone to love their mothers and stay out of trouble."

"We don't blame you, Margaret," Tom said, softly. "What kind of dimwits do you think we are?"

"Oh, I just knew you were going to say that," Margaret said. "Still, on some level, I think you do blame me. You left your own, sweet world — where everything was simple and you knew your way around. Then you came to see me. And here you are now in my world. I'm your hostess, taking you around New York City in 1984. Showing off my town and my time. And you are appalled. Who else are you going to blame?"

"It's not all bad," Tom said.

"No, just most of it."

"No, not even most of it," Tom said. "I think things are better now. Don't you guys?" He looked at Alfie and Gordie, who nodded on cue. He thought for a moment. "Yes, I really do. They're better on the whole of it. People live longer for one thing. Don't they?"

"Actually, they don't. Not beyond a certain age. More infants grow up to be adults. And fewer adults die of the diseases they died from in your day. Now it's wars, automobile accidents, murders, and in some cases, new diseases."

"Well then," Tom continued, "people are less ignorant than they used to be. They're smarter and more cultured."

"And more spoiled," Margaret said. "I think people are softer, less self-reliant than I remember. But maybe I just don't remember. When I was young . . ." She paused. "I was so young, that I didn't pay proper attention." She laughed and so did the boys.

"The world is still the world, isn't it?" she said.

The boys agreed, although they weren't sure precisely what she meant. When Margaret thought about it, she wasn't too sure herself. She only knew that, having voiced her unreasonable guilt, it went away.

"You know what you guys need?" she said in genuine good spirits. "You need to see the elegant side of New York. Lord only knows you've seen enough of the grubby side."

"Whoa," Gordie said, hanging on to the arms of his chair as if it were moving too fast for him. "I don't know about elegant. I'm just a farm boy."

The other three laughed.

"No, I'm serious," Margaret said. "On Sunday, let's go see some nice things. Let's start with . . . " She thought for a moment. "Let's start with a brunch at the Palm Court."

"What's a palm court?" Tom asked. "I never heard of a palm court, but I once ate at a tennis court."

Everybody laughed.

"You goofer," Margaret said.

Tom looked at her soberly, as did the other two.

"What's the matter?" she said. "What did I do?"

"You called me a goofer. That's what you used to call me in Cobblers Eddy. When you were Maggie."

Margaret thought about it for a moment, then shrugged. "That's interesting, isn't it?" she said. "Stand up, Gordie. I think you need a new pair of pants. Those are too small."

"That's fer sure," Gordie said. "And this is the biggest pair I've got."

"Tomorrow, we'll get you a pair that's big enough. A city this size ought to have at least one pair of trousers that will fit you." She looked back at Tom. "What else should we do?"

"See the Statue of Liberty," Tom said.

"No," Margaret said. "There's plenty of time for that. Besides, you wouldn't like it. They're restoring it. I saw something on TV the other day that they were removing the torch. There was scaffolding everywhere. It looked like a ruin. Anyway, what are you? A tourist?" She rubbed her chin. "No, I think some place mystical, like . . . "

"Grant's Tomb," Alfie said.

"No," Margaret said. "How about St. Patrick's Cathedral?"

"Isn't that a Catholic Church?" Alfie asked.

"Yes."

"Can we go there?"

"Sure."

"What else?" Gordie asked.

"I don't know," Margaret said. "That ought to do for starters."

Chapter Twenty-Three

The next Sunday morning, the three boys followed Margaret through the revolving doors of the Plaza Hotel, across the lobby and into the Palm Court. Margaret thought of her all too infrequent trips to the court as mini vacations — like stepping from the humid bustling streets of Manhattan directly into a cool, calm tropical retreat. She was transformed by the splendor of the court with its vaulted ceiling, its white wicker furniture and the profuse, lacy palms that tied it all together. And to complete the mood, a man in a tuxedo sat straight backed at a massive grand piano filling the courtyard with soft music.

She watched the boys drink in the ambiance. Surely this was a part of New York they had no idea existed. "The best is yet to come," she said with a wink.

Although the court appeared to be full, they were seated immediately at a round white wicker table where they could view the entire court in all its tropical elegance.

Margaret ordered eggs benedict, and Alfie ordered a filled French crepe. The other boys, somewhat overwhelmed by the menu, followed Alfie's lead. When the waiter left, they asked him what a crepe was. Alfie shrugged. "I don't know."

"Are we supposed to eat these here or take them with us," Tom asked, nodding toward the four miniature jars of marmalade and strawberry preserves in the center of the table.

"They're for your croissant."

"My what?" Tom said.

"Croissant." Maggie said using her best French pronunciation. "These are croissants," she said sliding the basket of rolls closer to him.

"What did you call them?" Gordie asked.

"They're croissants."

"You talk funny," Gordie said.

"It's French. They're a French pastry."

Margaret was a little apprehensive that the boys might be put off by the Palm Court; that everything might seem strange, confusing, and unnecessarily formal to them. But the court's emphasis on service put them at ease. Waiters anticipated their every need, invited them to the buffet table and, later, the dessert table. They were there when the boys arrived to make their choices and then carried their choices back to their table, arriving as if by magic before the boys did.

Margaret squealed with delight to find a truffle in her eggs benedict, explaining to the boys that truffles are fungi that grow underground and are rooted out by French pigs. And, considered to be very much of a delicacy.

"How do you know so much about French stuff?" Tom asked her.

"I majored in French in college and I almost spent a year in France. I worked for a French company for a few years and I love the language. Oh, yes, the elderly couple next door, the Mayers, they're French and they don't speak much English. So I get plenty of practice."

"I wonder why Mrs. Moss's pigs never found any truffles," Alfie said.

"If they did, they probably et 'em," Gordie said.

Everyone laughed.

From the Plaza hotel, the four walked a few blocks to the cool cavernousness of St. Patrick's Cathedral. Margaret stuck her hand in the holy water and crossed herself in a manner the boys had not seen before. Instead of following suit, the boys walked to an altar built around a statue of St. Anthony. Margaret, in a very somber, almost hypnotic state, bowed her head, put a coin in the slot and lit one of the candles in front of the altar.

"What does it mean when you light a candle?" Alfie whispered.

"You light a candle and say a little prayer for someone who is lost or in trouble or who died," Margaret said.

"Does it help?" Gordie asked.

Margaret looked at all three lovingly and smiled. "Apparently it does." she said. "But sometimes it really takes a long time."

Tom put a quarter in the slot and stood there holding a thin stick with fire on the end of it, trying to think of someone to light a candle for. He thought of all of the people in Cobblers Eddy. His mind began to open to a whole area of consciousness that he just didn't want to deal with then. He blew out the fire without lighting a candle, then put it back, only to grab another stick and quickly light a candle. "That's for everybody," he said to himself and turned to catch up with the others who, by then, were leaving the cathedral. They stood just outside the door and looked down at a middle aged woman dressed in rags. She was sitting at the curb next to a hand lettered sign on corrugated cardboard that said, "My name is Sharon. I am hungry. Will you help me?"

All three boys bounded down the steps while reaching in their pants pockets for money. When they got close, they each put a dollar into her basket. They were struck by how dirty and sickly she was. Her face did not brighten up when they gave her a donation, as they expected it might. She handed them a poorly printed sheet. On it was a written plea asking people to write to their state legislators encouraging them to make some sort of accommodation for street people like Sharon.

"When we first arrived in New York and realized that we had traveled in time, I felt like a visitor," Tom said, as they walked toward Broadway. "It didn't seem real. People seemed like actors playing roles. It was very entertaining. And educational. But it didn't have anything to do with me. It was a foreign country. I mean, how can you expect me to get involved in a nuclear freeze? I don't fully understand what a nuclear is, let alone how to freeze one."

Margaret laughed. "I can understand your not getting involved at first. But eventually."

"Yeah," Tom said. "Pretty soon it'll seem more real to me." He motioned behind him. "That dirty old woman,

Sharon, makes it seem real. I noticed that I wished I was a real New Yorker so I could write to someone. It's awful being out of money and with no friends in New York City. I know," he said. "The three of us know. It happened to us."

"Yeah, just for one day it happened to us." Alfie said. "And it was awful."

"Yeah," Gordie said. "It was a nightmare. Think what it must be like for that poor old woman."

At Broadway, Margaret hailed a taxi and took the boys to the newly developed South Street Seaport, which was jammed with people. Gordie invited the cab driver, a cheerful Algerian national named, according to the certificate mounted on the dash, Fakir Mustafa, to join them. The driver declined with good cheer.

"This is so different from where we went the first night we were here," Tom said, as they waded into the clean, well dressed crowd of calmer people — not at all like the frenzied scene they had witnessed in Greenwich Village. They walked toward the seaport itself, past a small German band that had attracted a circle of onlookers, past the neat, neo-rustic shops, the expansive new Fulton Fish Market jammed with people and a seemingly endless variety of food stores and restaurants, and past a fat little street artist who was scratching very life-like caricatures into brass, copper, and silver colored metal sheets for five dollars each.

"This is crazy," Alfie said when they got to the huge sailing boats moored to the dock. "We go into the future to see ships from the past."

Margaret sat on a bench. "This old lady is getting tired. I think I've made my point. New York isn't all sweetness and light, but it isn't all — what did you call it, Tom? Danger and what?"

The boys sat beside her.

"Din, dirt, and danger," Tom said with a touch of embarrassment. "I take it all back."

"Anyway, if you guys have seen enough, let's take a cab back home," Margaret said.

By the time they got to South Street, there were no cabs to be seen and at least 50 people waiting for the bus.

"Humph," Margaret said. "So much for taking a cab."

They got in line at the bus stop. They couldn't fit in the first bus, but got in the one just behind it. They had to stand in the rear.

"This is really not such a bad way to see New York," Margaret said. "You get a chance to see the people and neighborhoods along First Avenue. There are a lot of tenements and public housing down at this end. As you go uptown, the buildings get bigger and less residential." She held onto the post and stooped to look out the window.

"Wouldn't you like to sit down?" Gordie asked.

"In a little while, maybe," Margaret said. "I'm okay for now."

People got on and off the bus at every stop. A thick, muscular, middle aged man paused just before getting off. "Watch your pocketbook, ma'am," he said to Margaret. "There's a pickpocket working this bus."

"What'd he say?" Tom asked.

"He said there's a pickpocket somewhere on the bus."

"Where?"

"He didn't say where."

"What did the man say?" Alfie asked as both he and Gordie leaned over.

"He said there's a pickpocket on the bus," Tom answered.

"Where?"

"I don't know. But watch your pockets."

"Who do you think it is?" Margaret asked Tom.

Tom looked around. "That guy," Tom said, nodding toward the a tall, young black man carrying a coat over his arm.

"Oh, Tom," Margaret said. "I'm so disappointed in you. Just because he's black and most of the people on the bus are white?"

"No," Tom said. "It's because he's carrying a rain coat."

"So?"

"It's not raining and it's hot as blazes. I think he uses the coat to hide his hands," Tom said. "What other reason would he have for carrying the raincoat?"

Margaret raised her eyebrows. "I can think of half a dozen. It's torn and he's taking it to his aunt's to get it mended. He left it at his girlfriend's and now he's taking it home. He thinks it might rain before he gets home from work."

The boys looked out the windows for a few minutes, then Margaret spoke again. "He has his hand in that man's pocket," she said excitedly to Tom. "Look, that man with the raincoat has his hand in that old man's pocket."

In a loud voice that could be heard throughout the bus, Tom said, "That man is picking your pocket."

People turned to look at him, but no one moved. "That man has his hand in your pocket." he said.

At that, the man with the raincoat raised his hands to the level of his face to show he had nothing in them.

The bus stopped and the old man and several others got off the bus. The man in the raincoat did not. Instead, he sat in a newly vacated seat right in the midst of Margaret, Tom, Alfie and Gordie. They were thunderstruck by his move, having expected him to get off the bus now that he had been exposed.

Just as the bus was ready to get underway again, Alfie pushed the back door open again, preventing the bus from moving. "Come on, we're getting off," he said. He pushed the door full open and stepped off.

"Wait a minute, Alfie," Tom said, but he got off too, as did Margaret and Gordie.

The bus left and they saw the round elderly man who was the potential victim. He was reaching into his back pocket.

"Did he get your wallet?" Margaret called to him.

"No," the old man said. "I was just checking it again to be sure I still had it. Thank you very much," he said, tipping his straw hat toward Margaret. He walked away.

"What did you get us off the bus for?" Tom said to Alfie. "If anyone should have gotten off, it was the pickpocket. We were in the right."

"That man was thinking terrible thoughts. Really awful," Alfie said. "He was a lot madder at us than we were at him. An' he was plannin' on doing something about it."

"Oh oh," Gordie said. "What was he goin' to do?"

"Are you sure you want to know?"

"No." Gordie said. "I'm not at all sure. Tell me."

"He had a razor." Alfie said.

"Okay," Tom said. "You don't have to tell us more. We were standing there in front of him and him with a razor. I think we can figure it out."

"His thoughts were dark. Very dark. He was really mad," Alfie said.

Now that they didn't have to compete with the crowds from the South Street Seaport, it was relatively easy to hail a cab for the rest of the trip home.

Later that evening as they were sitting around the table eating a supper Gordie had prepared, Margaret said, "You boys are ready, aren't you?"

"Ready for what?" Tom asked.

"Ready to take care of yourselves in New York City — or anywhere else for that matter."

"We sure are," Tom beamed, "In fact, Margaret, don't you think we ought to get jobs now?"

Looking up from her plate, Margaret said, "No, that wasn't what I meant. I just meant that today's incident with the pickpocket showed me that you are extraordinarily well prepared to take care of yourselves. You did everything right — a whole lot better than I did, I'll tell you. You spotted the pickpocket, you exposed him, and Alfie had the presence of mind to get us all off the bus. That's all I meant. Not that you should get jobs."

"But we can't keep livin' off you this way," Alfie said.

"You're not living off me," Margaret said. "We are simply engaged in a noble experiment here. And I'm having more fun with it than I've had since we rode Mr. Kocher's cows in Cobblers Eddy."

"But the expense."

"Not really. My mortgage payments are the same whether you guys are here or not. Heat and electricity are about the same." She thought for a moment, then cast an eye at Gordie, who was scooping mashed potatoes into his mouth. "Of course, my food bill has gone clear out of sight," she said with a mischievous grin.

They all looked at Gordie who was about to take another fork full. "I'm a growing boy," he protested.

"Okay. If you boys want to get jobs, you can. In Cobblers Eddy. It's time we went down there and took a look. It may seem like only a couple of months ago, but remember, you guys haven't seen the place since I have. Almost sixty long years have passed. We've all got some shocks coming. You more than me. I've had time to get used to change. You haven't. Cobblers Eddy is likely to be a bit of a shock to you guys — like seeing your pictures in the newspapers was to me."

The boys were quiet, then Tom spoke. "Why do we always get onto these really heavy subjects while we're eating? My stomach just shut off at the prospect of so many people I've known — including Mom and Dad — passing on."

"An' the rest of them getting old and probably forgetting us," Alfie added.

"You have to go." Margaret was vehement. "You have to face it. Staying in New York and pretending it's still 1926 in Cobblers Eddy is just playing make believe. The truth is . . ." Margaret took a deep breath, and held it briefly as she looked into the faces of the three boys. She exhaled slowly. "You know what the truth is," she said softly.

Tom pushed his half finished plate away from him. "Then let's do it now, tomorrow," he said. "Let's get on with it."

Chapter Twenty-Four

They did not leave the next day as Tom had suggested. It took almost a week.

Not knowing how long she would be gone, Margaret tended to over-prepare for the trip. She made arrangements with the elderly French couple next door to take care of her tropical fish, then asked the boys to move the tanks to the couple's apartment. She paid her taxes and estimated utility fees in advance and arranged with her bank to gain access to her account from Cobblers Eddy. She asked the post office to hold her mail until she sent for it, then, to be on the safe side, she arranged for her neighbor to collect the mail that would inevitably be delivered to her apartment anyway.

To keep the boys occupied as much as anything, she asked them to go to the library to find the current telephone book for Cobblers Eddy. "See if you can get an idea of its size and look through the names to see if you recognize anyone," she said.

The boys came back from the library all excited. "We found Gloria Baggins," Gordie explained. "She's the only one whose name we recognized. She has her own telephone number and everything. I'm real anxious to talk to her," Gordie said.

"When we get there, you can talk to her. But you can't talk to her on the phone," Margaret said.

"Why not?" Gordie asked.

"She wouldn't believe you when you told her who you are. She'd think it was a cruel joke," Margaret said.

"Then you call her," Gordie said.

Margaret thought about it for a moment. "No," she said. "I don't think so."

"Why not?" Gordie said.

"Because I don't want to," Margaret said. "It's been so long. She might remember me, but I doubt if she'd remember my name. She might misunderstand if I said I was coming for a visit after all these years. She might have changed."

After she had finished making all her other arrangements, Margaret got her hair done and, without telling the boys, she visited her attorney to draw up a new will leaving her estate equally divided among Tom, Alfie and Gordie.

Once that was done, she was ready.

Unlike the boys' trip east, this time all four were paying passengers who would ride in the comfort and dignity of a passenger coach. They sat four abreast with Tom and Margaret on one side of the aisle and Alfie and Gordie on the other.

As they looked out the windows, the platform at Penn Station seemed slowly, almost imperceptibly, to move backwards. "We're movin'. We're on our way," Gordie said as the train glided smoothly away from the platform.

"This train doesn't click clack the way the other one did." Tom said, "but `cept for that, I'd have to say trains haven't changed a whole lot since 1926."

"Yes they have," Margaret said. "They've gotten worse. Trains are not a priority any more. People drive their cars. Or they take a bus or an airplane. Trains are old and slow and expensive."

Tom was surprised. "Is that why we're taking one?"

"No," Margaret said. "It's just that they're sort of comfortable. And, when you're my age . . . "

"I'm older than you are." Tom said.

Margaret restated her sentence as if she hadn't heard him. "When you've been around as long as I have, Mr. Technicality," she said, pausing for effect, "you find the relaxed pace and gentle sway of a train ride rather soothing."

Alfie leaned across the aisle to Margaret. "Hey Margaret,

this is swell," he said. "This is the first time we've seen anything outside of New York. There's a whole world out here.
I can't wait to see what Cobblers Eddy looks like."

"I can," Tom said. "I'm really . . . what's the word,
Margaret?"

"Anxious? Apprehensive?"

"Apprehensive sounds good. What does it mean?"

"Anxious."

"Well, that's what I am," Tom continued, "about going
back to my home where no one even knows me. It isn't as
if we've been gone long. Just a couple of months by our
tally. I wonder if Froggie . . . " he looked at Gordie, then
corrected himself. "Gloria Baggins will recognize us. Or will
we have to tell her who we are?" He thought for a moment.
"Or, will we tell her who we are?"

"She won't know me, but she'll know you the second she
sets eyes on you," Margaret said. "We'll have to figure a
way to break it to her gently."

Gordie leaned across Alfie to join the conversation. "Do
you think they call her Gloria? I bet as soon as we left, they
went right back to calling her Froggie. I'll bet it hasn't been
too good for her. I'll bet they call her Froggie, and that her
voice is deeper than ever and that she's the town character." Frowning, Gordie folded his arms across his chest
and looked out the window as the train emerged from the
tunnel and he got his first look at the marshes of New
Jersey. "It's not fair," he said.

Margaret picked up the conversation again: "I keep
wanting to ask you guys about Cobblers Eddy today. What
it looks like, if Guy Cragle's store is still there. How the
mail is delivered these days. Where the gas stations are.
What kind of farm machinery they're using. Then I suddenly realize that you don't know any better than I do.
Probably not as well, because I've seen how small rural
communities change with the times. Television antennas
on roof tops, metal oil tanks attached to the sides of houses, propane tanks, junked cars in yards, aluminum siding,
farm ponds built for fire protection, that sort of thing.
Seven Eleven stores. Drag racing strips."

"What's a drag racing strip?" Alfie asked.

"Usually some kind of little dirt strip where kids race

their hopped up cars," Margaret explained.

"What's a hopped up car?" Tom asked.

"A hot rod?"

"What's a hot rod?" asked Gordie.

"Lord, this isn't going to be easy." Margaret shook her head. "One of the first things you guys are going to have to do when you get settled is get a driver's license. — Not you, Alfie. You're too young."

"You need a license to drive?" Tom asked.

"Sure."

"You mean all those crazies driving cars in New York have licenses?" Tom asked.

"Strange as it may seem."

"Even the taxi drivers?"

"Yeah, especially the taxi drivers," Margaret said. "Kinda makes you wonder what it's all for, doesn't it?"

"How much does it cost to get a driver's license?" Tom asked.

"Somewhere around $20."

"Aha," Tom said. "Then that's what it's all for. Multiply $20 times all the drivers in New York and you have a swell reason for requiring licenses to drive."

Margaret began to chuckle to herself.

Tom looked over. "What are you laughing at?" he asked.

"Tom, I'm surprised at you," Margaret said. "You've only been in 1984 a couple of months and already you're a cynic."

"I'm a cynic?" Tom said in mock indignation.

"You most certainly are," Margaret nodded her head. "In a remarkably short time, you have become suspicious, distrustful, pragmatic and, yes, cynical." She narrowed her eyes and thought about it for a moment. "You look for an insidious motive in even the most innocent everyday situation — like the issuing of driver's licenses."

The old woman smiled broadly and patted him on the knee twice. "I like that in a young man," she said with a mischievous wink.

The four maintained an easy banter throughout most of the trip. They shifted seats frequently so the boys could sit next to the windows as much as possible. The boys had never seen any modern countryside and precious little countryside of any kind outside Cobblers Eddy. The train wound relentlessly through the heavily industrialized areas of New Jersey and its inner city sprawl of old tenement houses. Tom asked Margaret if that was what her brownstone looked like.

Margaret, who generally liked Tom's sense of humor, was not amused. "Certainly not when we lived in it," she said. "Those houses are brick, not brownstone, and they are not very pretty."

After passing through Camden, Philadelphia, Baltimore and Washington, the train headed west through the green rolling countryside of Virginia, West Virginia, Kentucky and Ohio, stopping occasionally to pick up and drop off passengers. It crossed over the border to Indiana and stopped at Indianapolis, where they quickly changed trains, boarding a local that passed through Cobblers Eddy. Unlike the trip to New York, this time the boys got a fleeting view of Indianapolis where someone had closed and locked the door of the boxcar. Margaret, Tom and Gordie got excited at the prospect of being so close to Cobblers Eddy. Alfie sat in the aisle seat with his arms folded and said nothing. Margaret was sitting by the window next to him. "Are you nervous or excited at the prospect of returning to Cobblers Eddy, Alfie?"

The corners of Alfie's mouth turned down in a pout. "I want to go back to it the way it was," he said leaning his head on Margaret's shoulder. She put her arm around him and thought to herself that, despite all his experiences, Alfie was still a homesick 14-year-old boy who knew he was about to be swallowed up by the changes he would find in the Cobblers Eddy of 1984.

"An' I hear the music again," he said to Margaret's surprise.

"What music, Alfie?" Margaret asked.

"You what?" Tom yelled so loudly it could be heard throughout the coach. He jumped to his feet. "Oh no. You hear the damned music?"

Gordie said. "Oh no. No no no. What's going to happen to us now? This ain't no boxcar. We paid for our seats. What's going to happen?"

"I don't know what's going to happen," Alfie said. "All I

know is that I hear the music."

Margaret was bewildered. "This is the music you heard on your way to New York? You mean . . ."

"I don't know. It doesn't mean anything. I just hear the music. And I'm scared."

They looked around at the old parlor car. Everything looked all right. No changes had taken place. The car looked old — as it had since the start — but the people looked modern. Alfie looked at Margaret in horror. "I don't know. I don't know what it means," the boy said.

For a moment, Margaret looked bewildered, then pensive, and finally her eyes filled with tears. "I know what it means," she said softly. "It means I'm going to lose you again. And I just can't bear it. You meant more to me than anything in the world when I was 16. And the world just came to a screeching halt when you were lost. A light went out that never came on again until two months ago when you three showed up at my door. And, now I feel so certain it's over. I know you're going back. I know it as certain as anything I've ever known. You're going back and I'm just a crazy old lady on a train to no place."

She dabbed her eyes with a lacy handkerchief from her handbag.

"Margaret, you don't know that," Tom said gently. "Maybe it doesn't mean a thing. Maybe we'll all go back. Maybe none of us. Maybe we'll go forward in time, but we'll go together."

Alfie's eyes got red and he shook his head from side to side in anger and frustration. "I wish I didn't hear it. I hate it. God, I hate it. I hate it. I hate it. I hate it."

"I think I know what's causin' it," Gordie said. The others looked at him. "I think it's you that's causin' it, Alfie," he said. "As soon as you said you wanted Cobblers Eddy to be the way it was, you started hearing the music." He shook his head in frustration. "I know ya don't mean to do nothin' bad, Alfie, but you're the one what's causin' all this here grief. It's maybe not your fault, Alfie," Gordie continued. "Don't blame yourself. It's nobody's fault. But surer'n heck, it's you that's caused it first and it's you that's causin' it now."

After some moments of stunned silence, Alfie spoke:

"The music stopped. I didn't do anything. It just stopped by itself."

"You didn't do anything?" Tom half whispered. "You sure you didn't do anything? I'm thinking the same thing Gordie's thinking. You must be doing something. What were you thinking when you started hearing the music? And, what were you thinking when it stopped? Try to remember."

"I don't know," Alfie said. His eyes filled with tears. "Leave me alone."

"We can't leave you alone," Tom said. "We're almost there. You could separate us from Margaret so's we'd never get back together again."

Alfie sobbed on Margaret's shoulder. "I don't want to lose you again," he said to her.

"Oh, dear me," Margaret said. "This is incredible. You boys really think . . . "

"I was picturing us jumpin' from the train," Alfie said. "But it was more than picturing it. I was making it up. Sort of like an invention. Like dreamin' where you make the dream instead of havin' it just happen."

Margaret's jaw dropped. "You can do that?" she said.

"What were you thinkin' the second time? When the music stopped?" Tom asked.

"I put a TV aerial on the general store and imagined I didn't know anyone in town."

The others stared at him in disbelief.

"It's more than just imagining, though," he continued. "I sort of let the town fill up with people I didn't know." He shrugged. "You know. The way you do when you imagine things sometimes."

No one said anything for a moment, then Tom spoke. "Alfie," he said softly, "I don't think other people do that."

"Least ways, not like you do," Gordie added.

"Oh, my good lord," Margaret said falling back to her seat. "Ho Lord. You really did . . . Oh Alfie, you sweet, innocent little boy."

"I think I kinda made the music happen, too. Not exactly, though. It's like a tune you can't get out of your head. That is, I didn't invent it. An' I thought everyone could hear it. But there was something very funny about it."

"Alfie, I have to ask you something very important," Margaret said.

"But I didn't know I was makin' it up . . . I mean not exactly. Not any more than anyone else does."

"I know Alfie. Now listen to me. How much control do you have? If you start picturing something, can you stop? Do you think you can recognize what's about to happen before you make it happen? This is very important, Alfie." Her voice broke slightly. "I don't want to lose you boys again."

"I didn't know, Margaret. Honest. If I had known . . . I mean, it never would have happened. I never tried to stop it because I didn't know I could. I didn't even know what was happenin'. I'm still not exactly sure."

"Alfie, you're going to have to be very careful from now on," Tom said. "If you ever ever ever hear the music again, you've got to stop it." He looked deep into Alfie's moist eyes. "Now that you know, Alfie, you can't ever let it happen again. Not ever."

Alfie's voice was thin and whining. "I know Tom. I promise. Right hand up to God and hope to die."

"Gosh, Alfie don't say that," Tom said. "Be careful what you hope and wish and imagine."

"Oh no. That wouldn't happen. When anything I imagine happens, I can tell the feelings. Like when we were in the boxcar and I got sick, remember? I had a fever at night. I dreamed that it took us so long to get to New York that Maggie would be old. I probably told you about the dream."

Margaret raised her eyebrows and cocked her head. "A dream?" she said.

"Yeah, but it whirled around in my head because I was sick an' all. I mean, it wasn't an ordinary dream."

"I should say not," Margaret said.

"I don't remember your telling me."

The four of them calmed down and tried to talk about other things. Or not to talk at all. Margaret was able to force herself to admire the Indiana scenery she hadn't seen since she was a girl. It was then the conductor walked down the lenth of the car nnouncing the next stop was Sizerville. Maggie stopped him. "You're not stopping at Cobblers Eddy? she said.

"No Ma'am," he said, "The train only stops at Cobblers Eddy if there's a passenger pick-up or if a departing passenger makes arrangements first."

"But we want to get off at Cobblers Eddy."

"Sorry Ma'am, You'll have to take a cab from Sizerville back to Cobblers Eddy. I'm really sorry. That's the best we can do at this time. Next time you buy a ticket, you may want to specify that you want to disembark at Cobblers Eddy. They'll be happy to oblige you. I'm sorry, Ma'am.," he said continuing up the aisle.

Tom looked around the coach. "Everybody looks like 1984, Margaret. That's a good sign."

"Oh, I suppose you're right," Margaret said. "How silly of me to worry about being separated again. An old lady's prerogative — to be silly."

The train slowed down to a crawl as they went around the bend at the boundary between what had been Maggie's father's farm and Jim Kocher's farm.

The boys ran out to the platform steps between cars. Margaret followed. "Are you thinking of jumping?" she asked incredulously.

"No point in riding all the way to Sizerville then back again," Tom said.

"But I can't jump," Margaret replied. "I'd kill myself."

"Oh golly," Tom said. "I didn't mean for you to jump. You can go to town and get a ride back to Cobblers Eddy. But for goodness sake, don't jump."

"Okay, okay. I won't. I won't. Don't forget your clothes bags," she said.

Each of the boys gave her a hug and a quick kiss, then peeled off the train like paratroopers. It reminded the old woman of countless World War II movies she had seen. As Tom jumped, he called back, "We'll meet you at Guy Cragle's store."

Guy Cragle's store was a relic from 1926. Did the boys fully realize what year it would be when they landed? She ached as she waved to the boys. They got smaller and smaller as the train took her farther and farther away from them.

Then a thought that seemed more like a certainty occurred to her. She would never see them again. She knew it. She would go to town and hire a taxi for the long ride back to Cobblers Eddy, and when she arrived, no one would have heard of the boys. The boys would have disappeared back into her past or her mind or her memory — wherever it was they had been all these years. She just knew she was seeing them for the last time in her life as they waved and got smaller and smaller and smaller.

The train began to pick up speed again, and Margaret had a fleeting wish that she had jumped, brittle 74 year old bones and all. She could still see the boys. They were waving goodbye to her.

Then she jumped.

Chapter Twenty-Five

As soon as her feet left the platform, Margaret was seized by panic. The wind was fierce. She felt herself whirling through space like a cannonball. "You crazy old lady," she sputtered with contempt, "you just killed yourself." She rolled backwards end over end. Her long skirt blew over her head to block he view. She flailed at the dress, trying to get a peek at home before the millisecond of pain she was sure would end her life. Now the panic was replaced by a kind of wild eyed excitement. She laughed wryly. "I'll die at home without ever seeing it." She fought the dress and felt herself propelling backwards at break neck speed. "One look," she pleaded.

Time seemed suspended. She crammed a thousand thoughts into that brief moment. She thought about the boys who had jumped just moments before. Would they find her body? Or would they land in 1926? Or some time in the 21st century? Or did she imagine the whole thing? Maybe she was crazy. Did crazy people know they were crazy? Or maybe this was the way one died — full of insane experiences that one never gets to tell to another living soul. "I don't know," she answered herself. "I never died before." She laughed at the ludicrousness of her own jabber. But the wind was so strong and her backwards movement so rapid she couldn't hear her own laughter.

She continued to fight for a look at the ground, but her dress seemed to have a will of its own — a will determined to deny her that last, precious look.

She was aware that she had been in the air an impossibly long time rolling over and over backwards, the click clack of the train echoing in her ears.

Then she hit with an awful crack, taking the full brunt of the impact with the hard ground on the flat of her back. She felt paralyzed and couldn't breathe. The darkness of her dress was replaced by a blinding aura of color. She was paralyzed and yet had an expanded sense of strength and joy.

Chapter Twenty-Six

The train was moving so slowly when Tom jumped that he landed on his feet and, after a few slowing strides, came to a stop. He turned to see Alfie and Gordie jump, then turn to wave at Margaret who held a handkerchief to her face in a gesture of grief as she and the train began disappearing into the distance. Finally, Margaret was so far away she could be recognized only by her dress. Tom had a fleeting feeling that he would not see her again, that he should have stayed with her. Then it happened.

The flapping dress leaped off the platform and whirled recklessly through the air before plummeting out of sight. He gasped, as did the other two, then lit out like a shot toward the spot where the figure had disappeared into the tall grass. Gordie was not far behind. But Alfie could not keep up.

"Where is she? Where is she?" Tom screamed in panic as he and Gordie zigzagged through the high grass looking for the exact place they had seen the flapping dress plummet to the ground.

He looked around and saw his brother Alfie staring dumbly at the ground.

Alfie looked up at Tom. "I'm sorry, Tom," he said. "I know I promised, but I just had to try it once on purpose."

A lump came to Tom's throat. All he could think of was that the old woman had been so mangled by the jump that Alfie was frozen by the sight.

"Look," Alfie said as Tom approached.

Tom pushed the bushes aside. He stopped in his tracks

and gaped. His jaw dropped, and his eyes filled with tears as he viewed the form amid the tangle of grass and weeds.

His mouth hung open as he reached down to the gasping figure fighting for air at his feet.

It was Maggie.

He helped her to a sitting position as she began sucking air at a more moderate rate. She looked at her hands, then glanced at her bare legs and her work shoes. "Whhhat?" she said.

Alfie looked down at her and answered her question in a low and somber voice: "You're Maggie again."

The expression on Tom's face changed from disbelief to unrestrained joy. "You're . . . " he said, choking back tears. "You're Maggie again." He started to laugh. "You're Maggie again. You're Maggie again!"

"Give me a chance to catch my breath," came a voice even sweeter and more beautiful than he remembered.

"Are you hurt? Can you stand up? Huh? Are you all right?"

"I think I'm okay. Just let me sit here for a minute. What happened? I had the wind knocked out of me. I feel a bit strange."

"I'm not surprised," said the shaken teenager, "I think you just swapped bodies."

"Now Tom," Maggie said. "You know that's not possible. Help me to my feet. I want to see if I can stand."

With the help of Tom and Alfie, she rose to her feet and took a couple of wobbly steps. Tom steadied her, then gave her a long, tight hug. "Maggie, Maggie," he said. She laughed that wonderful lilting titter he remembered so well.

Alfie pried them apart enough to join in the hug, then Gordie came rushing over crying "Maggie, you're okay, you're young, I love you." He put his arms around the other three and they danced around until they fell, giggling and laughing and crying hysterically, on the ground.

"If the folks in my office could see me now," Maggie said, and they all roared with laughter.

"I can't believe you're here," Tom said. More laughter.

Maggie stood up and pulled out a stalk of timothy hay. "Ahh," she said, sticking the stem in her mouth. "I haven't had one of these for nigh on to 58 years." They all laughed as she made an exaggerated display of eating the hay.

Her jaw began to quiver, and she spit out the hay. Her eyes filled with tears. She reached out and grabbed Tom, pulling him to her. "Come here, Alfie, Gordie," she said. She put her arms around all three and began to weep into Tom's shirt. "I'm sorry," she said. "I just can't help it. It's just that." The crying took over. She shook her head. "I'm sorry," she said. "I thought I was going to lose you again." She gave them another squeeze. "I may never let loose of you three guys," she said, giving them one last squeeze before releasing her grip.

"You're young again, Maggie," Tom said almost gravely. "I don't understand." He looked around. "Alfie," he called.

Alfie was hanging back. "What?" he said.

"What's happening, Alfie?"

"I I didn't know what to do. She jumped an' . . . I know I promised, but I didn't know what else to do. And I didn't even know it would work. I never did it on purpose before. She'd have been hurt real bad. I was afraid."

Gordie slapped his forehead with the flat of his hand. "Gollee!" he said. "You done that? You made Margaret young again jes' like that?"

"Oh Alfie," Maggie said.

"I'm sorry, Maggie," Alfie said.

"Sorry?" Maggie said. "Don't be sorry. You probably saved my life. Gave me back my youth."

Just then, Jim Kocher's cows, which had been grazing on the other side of the field, ambled on by, the high, straight back of Echo rising from the midst of the small herd.

"That's Echo," Tom said pointing to the herd. "Isn't that Echo, Alfie?"

"Yeah, that's Echo."

"What in the world is Echo doin' here?"

"Ah, I don't know. She goes where the rest of the herd goes, I guess."

"But in 1984?"

"This isn't supposed to be 1984. It's supposed to be 1926." He stared for a moment, his brow furrowed as he tried to understand his brother's concern. "You thought this was 1984 and I could give Margaret Stone Maggie's body?"

"Didn't you?"

"No," Alfie said with some indignation. "How in the world do you think I could do that? I just brought us all back to 1926. Simpler that way." He seemed satisfied with the logic his explanation.

Tom thought for a moment. "Actually, it's better that way, isn't it?"

"I like it better," Gordie said.

"I like it a lot better," Maggie said. "Indeed I do."

They walked for a few moments in silence. "Echo. That's the cow I rode, isn't it? I forgot his name."

"Her name," Tom said.

"Right. Her name," Maggie said.

"Look up there at that big rock under the maple tree," Gordie said.

"Hot diggety!" Tom said.

There were four jars and four one quart berry baskets on the rock.

"What?" Margaret asked.

Gordie said, "Them's the baskets and jars we used for our picnic the other, er, day. I mean year."

"Oh, my." Maggie said. "This is going to be hard. I'm supposed to know the significance of jars and baskets on a rock?"

"No, but we do. About two months before you went to New York, we had a picnic and left our jars and baskets here. We think that's what day it is. You rode Echo, that day."

"An' the train came by and we all jumped in the boxcar and danced," Alfie said.

The four sat on the rock. Tom picked up a glass mason jar and inspected it. "It's probably about June 23," he said, "and about time we were off to slop Mrs. Moss's pigs."

"You know," Maggie said, "It's no longer you guys who have the problem. It's me. All this is a few months old for you. It's nearly 60 years for me. I'm going to need some fast coaching from you guys." She put her hands to her cheeks. "Good lord. I'm going to see my parents tonight." She sat down on the grass. "What'll I do?"

"Right now, I think we'd better slop Mrs. Moss's pigs." Tom reached for Maggie's hands and brought her back to her feet.

"Must we?" she said. "I don't even remember how to slop pigs."

Gordie spoke. "It ain't exac'ly one of your more complicated chores, Maggie. We'll help you."

With Alfie and Gordie in the lead, the four young people hiked leisurely over the hill toward Mrs. Moss's house in the village.

"I can use all the help I can get," Maggie said. "I'm not kidding. You guys better stick real close to me. It's been a long, long time." She shook her head as she walked. "A long, long time. Every time we meet someone I knew, tell me their name. And keep explaining what everything is." She pulled out a stem of timothy hay and stuck the succulent end in her mouth. "And when I know something, but don't know I know, tell me I know." She chewed absently. "I want to act natural."

"Then you better not talk much, Maggie," Tom said.

"Why not, for heavens sake," Maggie said. "I don't want people to think I'm dumb. Or rude."

"You have a New York accent. And you put your words together like a 74-year-old."

"But I don't. I've always had a charming country drawl. People tell me that all the time."

"Trust me, Maggie. You don't sound right for Cobblers Eddy in 1926."

"Mercy me," Maggie said.

"Teenagers don't say 'Mercy me,' Maggie."

"What do they say?"

"Gee willikers."

"Oh dear. My folks are going to notice in a minute."

"Yes they are."

"But I can't tell them the truth. They'd never . . ."

"No they wouldn't."

"So what will we . . .?"

"Not we," Tom said, "you."

"What will I do? People will think I'm strange."

Tom stopped walking and stopped Maggie too. "Maggie," he said, holding both her hands. "You *are* strange. To quote what you said about us when we showed up in New York, `you have done something highly unusual.'"

"So what am I going to do?"

"Nothing, as far as I can see. Just let people, including your mother and father, think you're a little strange. You know, it's not everyone who jumps off a moving train and lands 58 years younger than she was when she jumped. Let's face it, Maggie. People in Cobblers Eddy are going to think you're strange. And, there's not a blessed thing you can do about it because you are. Strange."

Maggie smiled, then kissed Tom on the cheek. "Well, the proof is in the pudding, Tom," she said. "Do you think Mrs. Moss will notice the difference?"

"Ah come on," Tom said. "Mrs. Moss is as old as dirt. That's not a fair test. She'll be easy to fool."

"You think?" Maggie said. "If I can fool her, I ought to be able to fool the rest of Cobblers Eddy," Maggie said, adding "It's difficult for a young person to act like an old person. They've never been old. But old people have been young. They can be very convincing." She winked mischievously. "Just watch me."

Chapter Twenty-Seven

"Where did these gnats come from?" Maggie asked as they continued down the hill toward Mrs. Moss's. She tried to shoo them from her face. "They want to get in your eyes, your mouth, your nose."

"They're hungry," Tom said. "Don't you remember the gnats? Boy, you have been away a long time. Sweat and gnats are what summer is made of."

"I guess I didn't pay much attention," Maggie said.

"Do you remember the little flies that buzz around your head?"

"Vaguely."

"Do you remember horse flies?"

"Yes. I do."

"Were you ever bitten by one?"

"No. I don't think so. Was I?"

"Of course. Everybody was. How could you grow up in the country and not get bit by a horsefly?"

Maggie shrugged. They walked in silence for a few minutes. Maggie sensed an awkwardness between them that made talking difficult.

"Tom," she said. "Do I make you, uh, uneasy?"

"Do I act like I'm uneasy?"

"No."

"That's because I'm not."

"Why not? I'm more than four times your age. I've seen nearly 60 years you haven't seen. I've had a lot of experiences you haven't had."

"I know."

"I was married once," she said. "I had a son who lived to be older than you are now."

Tom said nothing, at first. Then he smiled.

"Why are you smiling?" Maggie asked.

"I was just thinking what a difference a few minutes can make. When you looked 74 — when you were Margaret — I would have thought nothing of your being married. And having a son. I think you told me about it, in fact. Your husband, Mr. Stone, was a drunk, wasn't he?"

"An alcoholic, yes."

"And, you had a very bad time with him. I remember your telling us." He looked at her again and smiled. "But when you, as Maggie, tell me the same thing, it's hard to picture it."

"But."

Tom held up his hands. "I know, I know. It's true. But it still doesn't seem real."

They walked in silence for a few moments.

"And that's why I was smiling," Tom said. "I know it's true, and I still don't believe it.

They continued to walk, then Maggie spoke. "Doesn't that sort of get in the way? Even though you don't believe it?"

"No."

"For heaven's sake, why not?"

Tom took a moment to collect his thoughts. "Because," he said at last, "there's one thing that never has changed and never will. You're Maggie, a one of a kind very special person." He didn't look at her, but she kept watching his face. "You were Maggie when you were 74 years old in New York. You were Maggie for the 58 years you had that we didn't have. You're Maggie. Always. And I trust you. More than anyone else. And I always will." He finally looked directly into her eyes and said, "Nothing else matters."

They continued to walk across the fields. "What was your son's name?" Tom asked.

"Tom," Maggie said.

"Figures," he said.

Maggie smiled to herself because, in that moment, a sense of joy returned to her that she had not known for more than half a century.

Chapter Twenty-Eight

Youth came back to Maggie in a rush of surprises. It was not as she had remembered it. Nor as she would have imagined it to be. The sights she saw and the sensations she felt all seemed in different proportion than she had remembered.

She would not have guessed, for instance, that her sense of smell would take over as it did from her other senses. The amalgam of aromas — fresh cut hay, distant barn smells, weeds, wild flowers, her own perspiration, the moist Indiana soil and leaves, wet grasses, the dampness of the brook bed — they all seized upon her lungs in a bouquet that was intoxicating. Her own nostrils became a miniature time machine that sent her zooming back to her girlhood on her father's farm — which was, incomprehensibly, precisely where she was.

She touched the tip of her middle finger with her thumb. Her fingers were more sensitive, yet more firm. Her feet were better padded against the rubbing of her shoes than she had expected.

She had forgotten the sound made by feet walking across a field of clover — how the stems of the clover clung to her shoe laces until broken off by the force of her forward stride. She heard the soft rustle of the wind, and on it, voices from several farms away. And the monotonous chugging of Howie Dubray's Farmall tractor straining into some faraway task.

Finally, she was aware of the energy that propelled her. How effortlessly she strode with the boys through the rolling fields, leaped across the creek, ran up an incline. Her wind seemed a thing apart from the effort she was putting forth on her swift movement across the fields.

"So," she said to no one in particular, "this is youth, eh?"

The boys didn't exactly understand what she meant. The extent of her transformation — and the suddenness of it — had not yet struck them. But while they failed to react, Maggie was rather pleased at the melodic sound of her own youthful voice. It had a certain musical quality, she thought proudly.

Coming into and out of her line of vision in regular rhythm was her long, yellow hair. She took a handful and fanned it out with her finger tips. She had forgotten how tame it was, how choreographed. Each thick, straight strand seemed to line up obediently with the one next to it and each toss of her head made the strands fall in graceful rhythm and accord. It reminded her of a shampoo commercial she had seen a few nights before in her Manhattan apartment.

Chapter Twenty-Nine

They reached the gravel road and started down the hill. Maggie was surprised how familiar some sights were after so many years, how unfamiliar others. She remembered clearly, for instance, the massive oak at the crest of the hill and the wild cherry tree that stood by it. But beyond them, a farm house and barn nestled among fir trees at the end of a winding country road created a spectacular panorama she did not remember at all.

A German police dog on a long chain barked at them from the other side of a stone wall.

"That's Spike," Tom said. "The Goss's dog."

"Is that Mrs. Goss?" Maggie asked nodding toward a middle aged woman with a red kerchief tied around her head who was beating a carpet in her back yard.

"Yes," Tom said. "But you call her Viola. Everybody calls her Viola. And that's Mary Cragle," he said of a darkly tanned woman in work clothes sitting on the porch of a house across the concrete road.

"She looks like a man," Maggie said.

"She works like a man, too. Farms full time," Tom said.

Mary Cragle waved, and the four teenagers waved back. They turned right on the concrete road.

The box-like silhouette of a Model T Ford rose to the horizon and sped by. The boys waved to the driver, a straight backed man with a black, wide brimmed hat.

"Who was that?" Maggie asked.

"I don't know," Tom said.

"Then why did you wave at him?"

Tom laughed. "This is Cobblers Eddy. Everybody says hello to everybody else. People are friendly."

"Hmm," Maggie said as she watched the Ford disappear into the distance. "Still," she said, "he looks an awful lot like a guy I saw running a shell game just off Times Square."

The boys all laughed.

"About how much does a Model T cost these days?" Maggie asked.

"About $400," Tom said.

"New?"

"Sure. The price comes down every year."

Maggie shook her head. "Unbelievable."

"Yeah," Tom said. "I suppose it would to someone who just last Sunday spent $100 for breakfast for four at the Palm Court."

"And that didn't include the tip," Maggie said smiling.

A small, sinewy man, deeply tanned, with a basket of groceries hanging on the crook of his arm, plodded along toward them. Maggie almost panicked. This would be the first person she met face to face. "Do I know him?" she said.

Tom looked at her quizzically. "That's Jim Kocher."

"*That's* Jim Kocher? Old Man Kocher whose cows we rode? Oh, mercy. What'll I say to him?"

"It doesn't matter what you say to him. He's too deaf to hear you. He'll only hear Gordie, because Gordie can be loud."

Kocher tipped his frayed straw hat as he approached. He stopped. "Good haying weather," he said in a high pitched voice. Then without waiting for a response, he added, "Yeah huh." He looked Maggie right in the eye and said, "How's your ma and pa?"

She spoke politely, saying "fine" with a slight curtsey, adding "I think" as she realized she hadn't seen them in their present form for more than a half century.

"Yeah huh," Kocher said.

Gordie spoke with more volume than usual: "How's your corn?"

"Oh, about this high," Kocher said, measuring with his hand to his waist. "Not so bad for this time of year. We could use some more rain, though."

"It's been a dry spring," Gordie said.

"Yeah huh," Kocher said. He tipped his hat and trudged on up the road.

Maggie watched him disappear around the bend. "That sweet old man," she said. "We've been riding his Holsteins and calling him `Old Man Kocher?' I can't believe it."

"You rode `em too, Maggie," Tom said.

"For the last time," Maggie said.

"Why?" Tom asked.

"Because he's such a sweet old man. How old would you say he is?" Maggie asked.

"Mid-70s," Tom said.

"That old?" Maggie shook her head in mock wonder.

Maggie was surprised at how few minutes it took to walk to the village of Cobblers Eddy. The village itself seemed small, the houses little, the distances between them short, and the roads narrow.

"That's Mrs. Moss's house up ahead, isn't it," Maggie said. "I recognize it."

Mrs. Moss had always been a woman of few words. And as she got old, she became even more so, seldom speaking aloud, preferring instead to nod, lift her eye brows, squint, glare, frown, and, on very rare occasion, smile.

She peered out her kitchen window as Maggie and the boys approached along the tar road. It seemed odd that Maggie had brought three friends. She didn't need anybody. Not Maggie. Something was clearly amiss. Mrs. Moss pushed open the screen door and, uncharacteristically, spoke: "Is you all right, child?" her voice crackled.

"Oh I'm just fine, Mrs. Moss," Maggie answered. She smiled and shot a quick, conspiratorial glance toward the boys.

The three boys shook their heads vigorously; too vigorously, Mrs. Moss thought. "She's real good," said the biggest one.

Unconvinced, Mrs. Moss went back into the kitchen and, stepping back from the window so she couldn't be seen, watched them. It was not unusual for Maggie to bring a friend or two, but never before had she let them help with the feeding. The old woman paced behind the curtains like a fox stalking a hen house. She took another look. Something wasn't right. That was Maggie sure enough. Who else could it be? That had to be Maggie.

Mrs. Moss had watched Maggie slop the pigs countless times before. The young girl was very particular. But today she seemed not to care. The old woman's eyes narrowed, her thin lips pinched shut. Glory be, she thought, those three young boys weren't just helping, they were doing all the work.

She watched as the biggest of the boys hefted a 10 gallon can of slop into position above the fence and splashed its contents carelessly into the pig trough on the other side. She waited for Maggie to chastise him, but Maggie made no protest. She just stood by and let the boys stir up the thick sour milk from the dairy and mix it with spoiled grain from the mill. She even let them feed the slop to the pigs and the boys seemed to be explaining it all to Maggie — instead of the other way about. Now the littlest fellow showed Maggie where Guy Cragel laid aside wilted produce from his general store. As if Maggie didn't know very well herself.

Feeding the pigs had always been a job Maggie jealously protected. And it looked to Mrs. Moss as if the boys — who had never fed her pigs before — were teaching Maggie how to do it. Indeed, she thought. They were clumsy young oafs without the least idea how to feed pigs proper. They actually spilled slop into the pig yard. How did they expect the pigs to get it off'n the muddy ground? And what part they got in the trough, they didn't spread along to both ends. They didn't put the meal scoop back on the nail, didn't even put the lid back on the milk can. And Maggie made no objection.

Was she sick? Mrs. Moss looked again. No, she looked healthy enough. And happy. It just made no sense.

The old woman busied herself in the kitchen, first refilling the kettle from the pump at the sink, then carrying it to the stove to simmer, then moving back to the window again to watch. She saw Maggie back away half a step when the pigs rushed to the trough. "Afraid of my pigs?" Mrs. Moss whooped. Was this some girlish trick to appear helpless to the boys? Mrs. Moss shook her head. No. Not very likely. Maggie was genuinely afraid of the pigs and acted as if she had never fed them before.

To test her suspicions, Mrs. Moss waited to see if Maggie carried an armful of kindling to the back porch as usual or if she'd ask the boys to do it. Bringing the wood was not a part of Maggie's chores, but she usually gathered up an armful from the woodpile behind the pig shed and carried it to the back porch. She laid it by the door so the old woman could keep her stove stoked without having to fetch the wood herself.

Maggie came straight to the back door. But she brought no wood, nor did the boys. She called though the screen door that the pigs had been slopped and she'd be back tomorrow. The boys nodded in agreement.

Mrs. Moss's eyes widened and her jaw dropped. The voice was Maggie's but the words and intonations were someone else's. Mrs. Moss was shocked. Maggie spoke distinctly and confidently. There was a smoothness, an un country dignity and sophistication in her voice as if she were playing a part in one of the plays at the Grange Hall. Except it was real — nothing a country teenager could imitate.

Mrs. Moss stared at Maggie for a moment trying to understand why the young girl was so unnecessarily explaining the obvious. And was it her imagination or was Maggie inspecting her as if she had never seen her before? This was Maggie's double, not Maggie. Mrs. Moss felt an eerie chill as she handed the young girl 15 cents and acknowledged her "thank you" with a stiff nod. As soon as Maggie and the boys turned to leave, Mrs. Moss rushed as quickly as her arthritis would allow to the front window to watch them disappear up the concrete road and out of sight. She shook her head.

After a supper of chicken broth and Uneeta biscuits, Mrs. Moss slid the kettle to the back of the stove. "Too hot for tea," she muttered. Then, using a cane for support, she moved to the front porch to escape the heat that built up in the house by late afternoon. She lowered herself into a sturdy oak rocker, then reached for a woven straw fan from the wicker side table and fanned herself as she rocked. She moistened her lips and looked far into the distance.

"That just ain't Maggie," she announced to the empty outdoors. "That child ain't Maggie. Couldn't be. That one don't even know how to slop pigs, for land sake." She rocked. "And she looks me in the eye. Maggie never did that."

Mrs. Moss pursed her lips in an expression of angry conviction as she stared straight ahead. "Young'ns her age don't never look folks in the eye.

"She talks different too. More slow. Says her words more plainer. She tries to hide it, but she's got a bit of a city sound to her. Now where would young Maggie come by such a thing?

"The only figurin' that makes any sense is that that ain't Maggie." She shook her head. "And that don't make no sense at all."

The small, solitary figure rocked on her front porch and stared, preoccupied, out into the horizon.

When daylight faded and the countryside took on the soft purple of twilight, Mrs. Moss struggled to her feet and, using her cane for balance, moved slowly inside to light a kerosene lamp.

"Two down," Maggie said as the four young people walked up the gravel road toward her house. "That wasn't so bad," she said. "I think they both accepted me all right."

"Who? The pigs?" Tom said.

"No, silly. Jim Kocher and Mrs. Moss."

"They were easy," Tom said. "Now you get to meet your folks."

Maggie's heart began to pound at the prospect of meeting her parents who, in her mind, had died years before. And the most ironic aspect of the meeting would be that they would have no idea what she had been through since she had seen them last. And there was no way she could tell them.

"Can you guys come over after supper?" she finally asked.

"Sure, what for?" Tom asked.

"We need to talk."

Tom looked at Alfie. "What did we do after supper last time we went through this?"

"I think we just bummed around. I did the dishes. Then we played cards or something."

Gordie spoke. "I know darned good and well what I did. I dug that foundation hole until it got dark, then I . . . Hey! Does this mean . . . ? Do I have to dig that hole all over again? I just started it last time at this time." He let out a long, low moan. "I hafta dig it all over again, don't I?"

"It's Alfie's turn to do the dishes, but I'll help him and we'll be over right after that," Tom said.

"I might not be able to make it because I gotta dig a big ol' hole. Again," Gordie said. "I mean I gotta dig it for the first time, again. And, my Dad don't like me wanderin' around after dark. He says somebody is likely to shoot me for a moose."

As they came around the bend, Maggie could see her house. It looked much smaller than she had remembered. And closer to the road.

Topsy waddled out from the rear of the house, sniffed Maggie's shoe briefly, wagged her tail, and waddled back. The three boys walked on by as she turned into the road toward her house.

"We'll see you tonight," Tom said, then whispered, "Good luck."

Chapter Thirty

"I'm not just talking about being well off," Maggie heard her father's voice, "Lots of folks are well off. I suppose we're well off for that matter. I'm talking real money. Honest to gosh really, enormously wealthy. I mean filthy, filthy rich. Rich enough that we could buy off the mortgage on this farm and flat out buy every other farm in and around Cobblers Eddy. And never feel a dent in our fortune."

Maggie let the screen door slam noisily behind her. The talking stopped and she walked into the living room.

"Hello Dear," her mother said.

Maggie choked a little as she tried to answer. Her mother, noticing nothing amiss, went on: "Did you bring back the jar and the basket from your lunch?"

"Oh no," Maggie said listlessly. "Sorry. I'll go get them later."

She was relieved to be able to talk. Without any conscious effort to do so, she walked over to her mother and gave her a big hug and a kiss. She could feel tears welling up in her eyes. She was aware of the smell of her mother and her youthful appearance. It swept her back in time so completely that she felt she had never left; that the 58 years had happened in the wink of an eye; or that they had never happened at all.

Then she was giving her father a hug and loving the smell of his perspiration.

"Are you okay, Honey?" he said. "What's the matter?" He gave her another hug, and she began to sob on his shoulder. Then Maggie pulled herself away. With her sleeve, she wiped a tear that escaped from her water filled eyes as she surveyed her parents.

"Oh Sweetheart. What's the matter?" her father asked gently.

"I'm just crying because . . . I'm so happy." she replied. "Such a lucky woman — uh, girl," she corrected herself. "You know how emotional girls are."

"Yes, but not you," her father said. "Are you sure everything's all right?"

She shook her head. "Boy, if it wasn't, it sure is now." She gave him another hug.

"Daughters are nice to have," he said, kissing her cheek again as they disengaged.

"Is supper ready yet?" he asked. "Do I have time to candle the eggs?"

"It'll be a few minutes. Maggie, if you're sure you feel all right, perhaps you could cut up the string beans." Maggie's mother said.

Supper was not easy because eating food was not easy. Maggie's stomach was in a knot from all the excitement. Her mind jumped back and forth between the here and now of having supper with the parents of her childhood and the reality of four hours ago when she was a 74 year old woman riding on a train. She talked very little, but kept eyeing these two precious people who had been lost to her for so many years. And they kept watching her. She was changed, and they knew it. Her voice was different, more controlled. She had a hint of an accent that reminded her father of one of his classmates from New York. She was uncommonly self assured, yet she was not talking very fluently at the table. When her parents talked about people and events, Maggie seemed not to know what or whom they were talking about.

"Are you sure you're all right?" her father asked.

"Yes, I'm fine, Daddy. Please don't worry about me."

After supper, her mother and father sat on the front porch talking. Maggie assumed it was about her father's plans for selling the farm and moving to New York. She hoped it wasn't about the changes they detected in her. She was grateful they had not mentioned the move to her yet.

As she was washing the dishes, she knew precisely in which cupboard each clean dish went. She laughed softly. "I can't remember people, places or events very well, but I know where every dish goes," she said to herself.

As she was finishing, she heard Alfie and Tom say hello to her parents and come in the front door.

"I'm in the kitchen. Come on in," she called to them. The three of them sat around the kitchen table. "Tea with cream and sugar, if I recall," she said.

"Milk, not cream," Alfie said.

Maggie snapped her fingers. "Darn," she said. "You know, you're right. It's a funny thing. Cream means cream — unless you're talking about adding it to coffee or tea, and then it means milk. I don't remember ever having real cream. Perhaps Carnation evaporated milk a time or two. But I don't suppose that's been invented yet." She looked at the boys. "How'm I adjusting, do you think?" she asked.

Alfie raised his eyebrows and watched her. Tom spoke: "Maggie, I haven't the slightest idea what you're talking about. They changed the meaning of cream? I didn't remember that."

"Oh, no no. That's not what I mean." She sighed heavily. "How do you make tea? Where are my Lipton flow through tea bags now that I need them? I don't suppose they've been invented yet, either."

"Tea bags have." Tom said.

"But nobody uses `em," Alfie said. "Least ways, nobody in Cobblers Eddy uses `em."

"Just put a couple of teaspoons of tea in the teapot and add boiling water," Tom said.

"Then what?"

"Then let it steep for a little while and pour it."

Once the tea had been served, Maggie spoke in hushed tones. "All right you guys. I need help. Making tea isn't the only thing I've forgotten. Before my parents come back inside, I want you to start telling me everything that's going on that I would know about if I had been here yesterday. I want names, places, exact events. I want to know who likes whom and who hates whom."

"Wait a minute," Tom said. "Don't say 'whom.' There's no

such word as 'whom' in Cobblers Eddy. Nobody knows about 'whom'. I don't even understand when you're supposed to say 'whom.'"

"Yeah, and you've been around," Maggie teased. "That's exactly right. You have to tell me things like that. And I need to know what the problems are. Who's going broke. Who's hard to get along with. What's going on in school. I want to know what we've done recently. If we went somewhere with somebody — anybody — recently, I want to know about it. I was a disaster at supper tonight. I just bluffed and bluffed and bluffed, and I don't want to have to do that again.

"By the way Tom, you were right. They did notice my accent. My father said it reminded him of a New York school chum."

Maggie sat on the edge of her chair, sometimes making little notes on the insignificant things the brothers told her. She was as interested in the small things as she was in the big ones. She wanted to know why Jenkins, at the feed store, limped. Where they got the ice from that was stored in the ice house. If old man Clinton was still alive. How long it took to get to town. The names of the people who ran the stand down in the village. How long ago the concrete road had been built. If the woman living with Jim Kocher was his wife or his sister. Who were the Bible toters and who weren't. Did anyone have eyes for her? When did school let out and when would it be starting again? How long did it take them to get to school and did Tom always stop by for her? What grade was Alfie in — and Gordie?

The boys just kept talking and she kept writing until, finally, Maggie's mother and father came in from the porch. Then she put away her notes and changed the subject. Maggie asked the boys if they wanted to play cards and, to her relief, they said no, that they had to get back because they had early morning chores to do.

After they left, Maggie was surprised how tired she was — and that she was not yet comfortable around her parents. She wanted to go to bed. Was it too early? She should have asked Tom what time she usually went to bed. Would her parents — especially her father — become even more suspicious if she went to bed too early?

She looked through the bookcase in the living room to find a book to read and discovered she had read almost everything on the shelf sometime between her childhood and 58 years from now. She found one called *Tom Knight's Diary* that she remembered from her childhood and thought would be interesting to peruse again.

"I'm going to read this upstairs," she said, kissing her parents good night. Using the hall light to see, she entered her girlhood bedroom, put the book on the wash stand, and took her gown off the hook in the closet. As she put on her gown, she wondered whether she usually left her bedroom door open or closed. "Probably open," she said aloud. She turned out the hall light and felt her way through the dark to her bed. Maggie's last conscious thought was to hope her New York neighbors wouldn't forget to feed her fish.

In her dreams, she was still 74 years old.

Chapter Thirty-One

Maggie's first view of the morning was the sight of her own foot sticking out of the covers. She watched it for a moment, not entirely sure where she was or whose foot she was looking at. She wiggled her toes, and the toes on the foot she was watching moved.

She jumped to a sitting position and looked at both feet. She looked at her hands, pulled up the sleeves of her long nightgown and looked at her arms. "Wow," she said under her breath and hopped out of bed. She quickly took off her nightgown and stood naked in front of the long, oval mirror. She looked at her tight, flat stomach. Her face. "Mercy," she breathed. She felt her small, firm breasts. She turned so she could see her buttocks and felt their contour with her hand. She swung her hips from one side to the other. "What a body I had. What a body I *have*," she corrected herself. She pivoted to look at her backside again. "Ohhh," she moaned.

As she quickly dressed, she thought about the difference in sexual patterns between rural Indiana in 1926 and urban New York City in the 1980s. "My kingdom for the pill," she said to the reflection in the mirror as she brushed her long, blonde hair. Then she quickly blushed. "I can't believe I said that," she murmured self consciously.

Overpowering excitement was swelling within Maggie. She could hardly contain herself. She wanted to jump and scream. She was sorely tempted to rush into her parents' room, kiss them and hug them and dump them out of bed. The air smelled good and the beauty of a new morning forming among the mist outside her window was breath-taking. This life was such a masterpiece of consciousness. It had to be preserved and enjoyed. Such a gift. "I think I'm drunk," Maggie said out loud. "I feel so high."

A few minutes later, she was tiptoeing down the stairs and out the back door. She put on her shoes and ran all the way to Tom's parents' farm, where she threw pebbles at Tom's bedroom window. Suddenly, the door opened. It was Tom's mother.

"Good morning, Maggie. You're up early. Tom's down in the barn milkin'."

"Thank you," Maggie said. She went to the barn.

"Hey, hot shot," she said to Tom. "Where's your father? You doin' the milkin' alone?"

"Maggie!"

"I've got to ask you something I forgot to ask you last night."

"What?"

"What are my chores? I don't remember exactly."

"Now let's see," Tom said, rubbing his chin. "You collect the eggs and candle them. Scrape up the manure in the stalls and put down fresh straw. Put the cows in the stan-chions and feed them. And help with the milkin'."

"Am I late?"

"Nah. Your dad doesn't start very early."

"Hey Tom."

"What?"

"Are you as high as I am this morning?"

"Gosh Maggie, I think I must be. I exploded out of bed this morning. I've never felt so . . . I've never felt so blessed. So much like I was in the middle of incredible beauty. I don't know how to say it. I just wanted to kiss and hug my parents. Alfie. The wall. The dog. The cows. The horses. Oh yeah, you feed your dad's horses, throw them some hay and brush them too. I feel," he threw his hands in the air. "Spectacular — no no, better than spectacular."

Maggie's eyes sparkled as Tom talked. "Me too," she said. "You know, I was really seriously considering dump-ing my mom and daddy out of bed onto the floor this morn-ing just because I wanted to be with them."

A serious expression came over Tom's face at the mention of Maggie's father. "Maggie, do you remember what the deadline is for your father's going to New York?"

"Deadline? What do you mean?"

"It's just a few weeks away, Maggie. The 30th of June. That's when he has to record some sort of document from New York at the county courthouse."

Maggie frowned. "We've got to talk about this, Tom. But I gotta do my chores now. Can you come over after you finish yours?"

"Sure."

"And, Tom, one other question: When do I get to eat breakfast? Before chores or after?"

"After."

"Phooey, Tom. This can't be heaven if you have to wait until after your chores to eat breakfast."

She left.

Chapter Thirty-Two

By the time Tom got there, Maggie was collecting eggs in the chicken house. "Hey, you're fast," he said. "You must have whipped right through those chores."

"I haven't done most of 'em yet. And I'm starved."

"Let me help you. How many have you done so far?"

"All but those last two . . . nest . . . house-like things. What do you call those things?" she nodded toward the double rows of ten little cubby holes that chickens climb into to lay their eggs.

"I don't think we call them anything. Nests, maybe."

"Do you know those ornery little creatures peck at you when you try to take the eggs out from under them?" Maggie said.

"That doesn't bother you, does it?"

"Heck no," Maggie said. "I'll wring their scrawny little necks if they mess with me."

"16 years old and 74 years tough," Tom said.

"I am pretty tough for a 16 year old country girl, aren't I?"

Tom scratched his chin and thought about it for a moment. "I don't know, Mag. You've always been pretty tough."

"Tell me about the timing for my father's big business deal."

"Okay. But what I'm telling you is what you told me — you know — before." He reached under a chicken and pulled out two white eggs, which he carefully placed in Maggie's basket.

"By this time, last time, your father had already told you about his plans. I take it he hasn't told you yet this time."

"Right. I think he might have last night, but all my focus was on this tremendous reunion with my parents — a reunion they didn't know we were having, I might add."

"Yeah, that must have been really something. I wish I could remember more of what you told me last time. I think it was the same day you rode Echo and we all rode the boxcar that he told you. And you told me tonight — that is, the first tonight at the strawberry social, not tonight at the strawberry social."

"Don't make it more complicated than it is. Just say the first tonight or this tonight. I'll understand."

"Okay. The first yesterday, I think that's when it was, he told you he needed some signed papers from New York by the end of the fiscal year, June 30th. He had to sign them, then get them registered at the county courthouse before it closed on the 30th. It was a squeaker, but you swiped Smokey Joe's horse almost right out from under him and got the envelope to your dad, and the two of you chugged on to the courthouse in his Model T, just making it before they closed."

Maggie giggled shortly. "Yeah, I remember swiping Smokey Joe's horse. He was such a sweet old guy. I bought him a whole carton of chewin' tobacco to make it up to him. Well, I don't see that we've got much of a problem. I'll just drag my feet, and Daddy will never get it to the courthouse on time."

Tom was frowning.

"What's the matter?"

"You don't remember the same details that Alfie, Gordie and I do. But these days are not the same as the first days were."

"I got up earlier this morning than I did the first this morning. And I felt so good, I did the chores for my dad. He slept longer, but still got started working earlier. That'll change every part of his day. Because he didn't have to wait until after chores to have breakfast, Mom made it for him earlier. And that will change her whole day. And it will change the days of everyone she meets and a lot of people she doesn't meet. There's a whole chain reaction to that one little deviation between this this morning and the first this morning."

"What are you trying to tell me, Tom?"

"I'm trying to tell you that, because I got up earlier this morning, the whole world changed."

Maggie looked at him thoughtfully.

"You can't count on anything being the same," Tom continued, "and if all you plan to do is drag your feet a little on June 30th, you could find yourself living in New York in a month anyway."

"Not me, Buster. There's no way this lady's going back to New York." She led the way out of the chicken coop, carrying a basket of eggs. "Wild horses couldn't drag me back."

"If your father went, you'd go. How could you stop it?"

"You just watch me. I'm staying here."

"You might not have a choice."

Maggie turned to Tom. "Look Tom," she said. "One always has a choice. You may not like the choice. Or you may not recognize the choice immediately. But you have a choice. If I don't want to go to New York, I'm not going. Period. Don't tell me what you and your little brother have figured out. I think by this stage in my life . . ." She shrugged. "You know what I mean. By now, I know how to keep myself from going to New York — or anywhere else I don't want to go."

Tom put his hands on Maggie's shoulders and turned her around to face him. He tried to pull her close but she resisted. She looked down at his hands.

Tom took his hands away quickly. "This is no good, Maggie, Mrs. Stone, Ma'am. Either you're 16 or you're 74."

"I'm 74," she said.

Tom looked at Maggie. He couldn't read her face at all.

He continued. "When I tell you that this time through is different than last time because we are different, I want to be listened to. I don't care if you're 74. You always used to listen to me. When we were in New York, you thought I was pretty wise. Now you're dismissing me. An adult dismissing a child. When I say you have to go if your parents go, you give me the benefit of your vast and awesome experience. `One is responsible for one's own destiny,' you say. `One always has a choice.'" He was imitating the authority in her voice.

She furrowed her brow. "Tom, I'm a retired career woman from New York. I've lived a full life. I have learned a good deal about myself over the years — and a good deal about human nature. The Maggie you knew no longer exists. She's been replaced by an old woman who simply looks like her."

Tom looked down at the ground. "If you're 74, you have no right to be as pretty as you are. I just want to hold you and hug you and carry on the way we did before you left," he said.

"Oh ho, Tom," Maggie said, tilting her head. "Now just a minute. No matter what I look like to you, I am really 74 years old. And you really are 17. If you think I'm going to pretend I'm 16 on a permanent basis, you're just plain wrong."

"But you really froze up when I touched you a minute ago."

"Touched me?" Maggie said. "You didn't touch me, you grabbed me like I was a sack of grain."

"So what's wrong with that? I always grabbed you. And you grabbed me. We weren't afraid to touch each other. You acted just now like you were . . . offended. By me. Golly, Maggie."

"I'm sorry, Tom. You're about the last person on earth I want to offend." She grabbed his hand. "Give me a little time to sort this thing out. I am most certainly 74, but in a lot of ways, I like the 16-year-old better. Let's talk about it later."

They reached the barn.

"What do I do with the eggs once I've collected 'em? Take 'em up to the house?"

"No, you take 'em to the apple cellar to be candled later. Here, I'll show you." Tom rubbed his chin. "On second thought, you better leave 'em there. You'll never get done if I have to show you how to candle eggs. Maybe your dad will candle 'em later."

She put them on an up ended crate in the dankness of the apple cellar. "That okay?" she said.

"Yes," Tom said.

"Now what? Breakfast?"

"No," Tom said, "The rest of your chores."

"Oh bother," she said following Tom into the barn.

Chapter Thirty-Three

Tom and Alfie rocked on the front porch swing, waiting for their parents to come out. "By our countin' of time, it's been almost five months exactly since we went to the strawberry social last time," Alfie said.

On his lap, Tom held a large basket of strawberry tarts, covered by a red checkered cloth. "We were only in New York for two months," Tom said.

"Yeah, but we were here for three months before we went to New York."

"Oh yeah, I guess that's right. It seems more recent than that," Tom said.

"I'll be glad when the three months is up," Alfie said.

"Why? Are you anxious to go to New York again?"

"Hah. I wouldn't go to New York again if you paid me. You couldn't even pay me enough to crawl into a boxcar again. I just mean it's going to be nice when we haven't been through the days before."

"Yeah," Tom said, rocking gently. "Actually, it's not as boring as I thought. The days aren't that much the same."

Alfie looked at him. "They're not?" he said. "I thought they were the same days."

"They are the same days. But things don't happen exactly the same. People are different."

"They are? I thought they were the same people. What do you mean, the people are different?"

"It's like . . . " Tom stopped rocking and leaned forward. "I don't know how to explain it. They don't do exactly what they did before."

"We don't do exactly what we did before because we're different. But everybody else is the same," Alfie said.

"They may be the same people but they don't do the same things they did before. Gosh, Alfie, you're as stubborn as Maggie. When we act different, we change everything. Think about it."

There was a moment of silence. "Okay, I thought about it, and I still don't get it." Alfie said.

"Okay. Let's say last time at the strawberry social you said hello to Jenkins. He says, `Eh? What's that, boy? Oh yes. Hello there.' And then he goes on about his business."

"So what?" Alfie shrugged.

"Okay, this time when you pass him, you're thinking about Margaret Stone's electric garbage grinder or something. And you don't say anything. So Jenkins passes without stopping and without interrupting whatever he was thinking about the first time. So he gets where he's going a little sooner and he is thinking different thoughts when he gets there."

Alfie looked at his older brother for a few seconds, cocked his head and said, "Doesn't that depend upon what he was thinking? And what difference does it make if he got wherever he was going a few seconds later?"

"It doesn't make a whole lot of difference, but the point . . ." Just then the front door swung open and the boys' parents swept onto the porch. Their mother grabbed the basket of strawberry tarts from Tom's lap. "I'll take those in the front seat with me," she said. "You boys get in the back."

Tom and Alfie looked at each other. "How much you want to bet we're the first ones there and Dad asks where everybody is?" Tom whispered.

Alfie snickered as the two boys got into the car and their father drove off. During the short trip to the church, the boys tried to muffle their laughter. Their parents ignored them.

A few minutes later, their father pulled up to the church lawn, yanked on the emergency brake, leaned out the window and pushed his hat back. "It never fails," he said, opening the door. He got out and walked around the car to his wife's side. "We're the only people here. Where is everybody?"

Alfie started to laugh. His father looked at him briefly, then turned away. Alfie pulled on Tom's sleeve and put his hand out. "Pay me," he said. "I told you people don't change. Only us."

Tom slapped Alfie's hand in payment, and got out of the car. "You don't get a cent, Buster. Last time he got out of the car first, then walked into the church yard. He came back to Mom's side of the car before he said anything."

"Did he really?"

"And he said it differently. I don't remember how, exactly," Tom said.

"But I don't get it. What made him change."

"We did, Alfie. See. That's the point I'm trying to make."

"But what did we do?"

"I don't know. I can't imagine. We giggled in the back seat, maybe."

"But he never said a word. He didn't even notice."

"Maybe it took us a bit longer to get to the car. Maybe it was something else."

Tom caught up with his mother. "Do you want me to put that on a table somewhere?" he asked her.

"No thank you, Dear. Here comes Marion," she said. "She'll take care of it."

"You're a little early," Marion said as she puffed up the hill wiping her hands on her white apron. "Just went down to the house to get cleaned up a bit," she explained.

"What time does this thing start, anyway?" the boys' father shouted across the lawn to her.

"When everybody gets here," she said, disappearing through the church doorway.

He turned toward his family and said in a confidential tone, "Hah, I've heard *that* one before. But it didn't start when *we* got here. Fix up this table, boys," he said. "Looks like we're the first ones here."

Alfie picked up a tablecloth, napkins, and some silverware and leaned over to Tom, "That's all different from the way he said it last time."

When Maggie arrived, she found Tom and Alfie and asked them to stay close to her during the evening. "You were right, Tom. People really notice a change in me," she whispered. "They say I'm quiet and think I'm worried about something."

"Are you?" Tom asked.

"I'm worried about *everything*," she said. "This is like performing in a play without having seen the script."

Despite such subtle changes, the scene looked to Tom and Alfie very much as it had a few months earlier. People drifted in, materializing rather than arriving. Daylight dimmed and darkness seemed to rise from the ground, with the sun still hitting some high clouds. A crude string of electric light bulbs suspended among the trees was turned on.

The church women busied themselves carrying a steady stream of food, plates and silverware from the church to the tables. Adults sat on wooden benches, mesmerized by the flames under a huge black pot suspended on a pole across two metal barrels. And Buck Baggins leaned against an apple tree explaining the workings of a tractor gear box to a rapt audience of five men.

"Where's Gordie?" Tom asked.

"He's around," Maggie said. "I saw him just a minute ago. What's all the urgency about?"

"You don't remember last time?" Tom said, shooting a knowing glance at Alfie.

"No," Maggie said. "What happened?"

"You'll see. Gordie put on quite a show," Tom said.

"Gordie did?" Maggie asked.

"You'll see," Tom said. He looked around. "Where is Gordie? It was pretty soon now that he and Buck Baggins got in a real loud argument."

Maggie shook her head. This was like watching a movie with someone who has already seen it, she thought. Except this was real. The events were really happening. Of course, she reminded herself, she had been through these events herself, but didn't remember them like Tom, Alfie and Gordie did.

"If you're lookin' fer me, you can stop lookin'," came Gordie's voice. They looked behind them to see Gordie hefting a huge tub of bottles of soda pop bobbing in ice water. A bottle opener dangled from a string attached to one of the handles.

"Hey, look what he brought for us." Tom said.

"Not fer you," Gordie said as he walked right past them to the small group of men listening to Buck Baggins.

He placed the tub on the ground at the base of the tree. Buck Baggins put his foot on the rim of the tub. "That's a good place for it, Boy," he said and continued his discussion.

When Gordie rejoined the group of young people, Tom was thunder struck. "What did you do that for? You ruined the whole thing."

Gloria Baggins, who had tagged along behind Gordie, smiled. "I think it was kinda nice. My pappy would have just asked one of us to go fetch him a drink," she said in her deep voice.

Tom glared at Gordie, frustrated that, because Gloria was there, he couldn't say more. Gordie had deliberately changed the tenor of the whole evening. He had side stepped the argument with Buck Baggins by making it unnecessary for Gloria's father to ask her to get him a drink. And what irked Tom more, perhaps, was that Gordie seemed proud of himself.

At the first opportunity, he went into a private huddle with Gordie. "What the Sam Hill were you thinking about, Gordie? Do you realize what you've done? Buck Baggins will go right on calling Gloria `Froggie.' And, you made big points with Gloria — and most everybody else — when you challenged him. You even made points with Buck Baggins himself." He threw up his hands in despair. "And now you throw a monkey wrench in the whole thing."

"I know. I done it on purpose."

"Why?" Tom asked.

"Cuz. I ain't no actor. I'd have looked real dumb tryin' to act like I was angry the second time — like I really was the first time."

"Why wouldn't you be angry the second time?"

"Cuz there was no surprise to it. The first time, he took me by surprise. I was thinking about what a swell girl Gloria was and how rotten it was that everybody didn't call her Gloria, then along comes her father at a gathering of folks from all over the area and he calls out so everybody can hear, `Hey Froggie, bring me a drink.' Geez, it still makes me a little mad, but I've had time to think about it now."

"But . . ."

Gordie put his hand on Tom's arm. "I couldn't have done it, Tom. I'm no actor. Believe me, at the end of tonight, I'd have looked like a durned fool."

Tom shook his head. "It ought to be an interesting evening."

"I gotta get back to Gloria," Gordie turned and left.

Tom returned to Maggie with a big smile. "Do you remember any of this?"

"Sort of," Maggie said. "All the strawberry socials over the years seem to blend. It's hard to remember which is which. I suppose I remember this one, but it's hard to be sure."

"Gordie was supposed to have a big, knock down, drag out argument with Buck Baggins because Buck called Gloria, `Froggie,' and Gordie didn't like it."

"Sounds vaguely familiar," Maggie said.

"Yeah, well it's not going to happen. Gordie decided not to do it. Says he can't pull it off when he knows what's going to happen."

"So?"

"So about this time, you ask me to go over and have a piece of strawberry shortcake with you so you tell me a big secret — which happens to be that you are going to New York with your parents. And I'm really, really crushed by the news."

"And?"

"And, let's get some shortcake anyway?" Tom said.

"Why not?" Maggie said, grabbing his arm in a manner more common in New York City than Cobblers Eddy. "Maybe we can eat it on the bench over there."

Tom cut two pieces and put them on plates. Maggie dripped chopped strawberries and syrup over them, then the two moved to the bench where Maggie sat down and Tom straddled the bench facing her.

He shook his head.

"What's the matter?" Maggie said.

"Nothing. It's the same old thing," Tom said. "I don't know whether you're Maggie or Margaret."

"I'm Maggie on the outside and Margaret on the inside," she said. "Sort of."

"I think I was more comfortable with you when you were all Margaret." Tom said. At least you were what you looked like, my Maggie plus 58 years. Now I don't know who you are."

"I'm still your Maggie plus 58 years. It's just that I don't look like it any more."

"Is that all? Don't you feel any different?"

"Yes, I do. It's true. I feel a lot different."

Tom turned and leaned back against the clapboard side of the church and pulled his feet up on the bench. He was encouraged by Maggie's tone. "How do you feel different — an' don't tell me you just feel younger and stronger."

Maggie thought for a moment. "I don't know, Tom," she said. "I just feel like a kid — sort of giddy and hopeful."

"Do you feel different about me than you did in New York? I feel different about you."

Maggie smiled. "I'll bet you do. And yes, I do feel different. Toward you, that is."

"How do you feel different?"

"Come on, Tom. That's not fair. I can't help the way I feel. I mean, what would you expect. I'm 16. That is, I've got a 16 year old body with 16 year old . . . " she paused for a moment, "hormones." She blushed.

Tom smiled.

"It's not funny. I've got a real problem."

Tom said nothing.

She grabbed his hand and looked into his eyes. "I'm a freak, Tom."

"You're no freak, Maggie," Tom said.

"But I am, damn it. Do you know who my boyfriend should be? Jim Kocher, that's who."

"Geez, Maggie. Don't be silly." Tom said.

"You think that's silly, eh? I'll tell you what's silly. I am. I'm silly — a 16 year old with a slight case of 58 years' additional memory."

"I love you, Maggie. And I don't care what age you are."

Maggie put her hand out as if to call halt. "Now just a minute, Tom. Don't tell me about love. I loved you throughout my whole 58 years. I named my son after you. I carried you in my heart. And I dreamed the impossible dream of getting you back. But don't you see? I thought you'd be like me. But you're not. You're still 17, Tom.." Maggie was silent for a moment. She looked at the ground. "I don't feel good about this, Tom. I feel like a pervert. Like a child molester." She looked up at him again. "I don't belong anywhere. If there are any other people like me, I don't know where they are."

"What do you think about Alfie?" Tom asked.

The abrupt change of subject irritated Maggie. "What on earth does he have to do with anything?" she said.

"If you don't belong anywhere, then neither does Alfie. Do you think he should only go out with girls that have natural knowing like he does? I mean when he's old enough?"

"Of course not, but that's different."

"No it's not," Tom said. "He's always dealing with special thoughts that no one else has. Or ever will have. Why is that so different from your special knowledge?"

"Because . . . " Maggie said.

"Do you think he should marry an Indian mystic?"

"Of course not. It's just that . . . well, I just don't see them as being the same thing. Let me think about it." She was silent for a few moments. "You really make a good point. Let me think about it for a while."

Chapter Thirty-Four

"How are you getting home," Maggie asked Tom as the two of them stood at the sink in the church kitchen washing silverware and drinking some of Marion's favored home made birch beer.

"I'm hopin' your dad will give me a ride."

"How did you get home last time?" Maggie asked.

"I didn't stick around to clean up after the strawberry social last time."

"Why did you stick around this time?" Maggie asked coyly. "So's you could be with me?"

Tom smiled back and said just as coyly, "No. I wanted to be with you last time, too. But I couldn't manage it."

"Why not?"

"Boy!" Tom said. "Who knows? It was different last time and I don't know exactly why. The least little thing changes everything. And most of the time, I haven't any idea what changes it." He picked up a dish towel. "I'm going to dry for a while, until we get caught up." he said.

"I don't notice any difference. But then, after 58 years, I don't suppose I would." She put a steaming handful of silverware on the counter. "Everything changes, doesn't it?"

"Yes," Tom said. "It does, Maggie."

"You think my father might be going to New York — even if I don't help him get to the courthouse, like I did last time?"

"Yes."

She looked directly at Tom. "Me too," she said. "I was a bit slow getting the idea yesterday when you were telling me about the whole world changing. But . . . " she paused, "Tom, this is one thing I don't want to take a chance on. What do you think we ought to do?"

"Make sure that letter doesn't get to your father. Just because it arrived late last time . . ." Tom let the words hang.

Maggie let out a long, low whistle. "Could the letter arrive a day early, do you think?"

"It could."

"Or Smokey Joe could be delayed until it arrived and take it with his regular delivery on Wednesday?"

"Maybe. Or the courthouse might stay open. Or someone might call from Cragle's store and ask them to wait for your father. Or the clerk might re-open the courthouse for a five dollar bill."

Now Maggie looked worried. "He'd do it for a lot less. Tom, we need a plan."

"And we need it bad."

The door to the outside swung open. "Maggie, Honey," Maggie's father said. "Will you hold the door for us?"

"I'll get it," Tom said, rushing toward the door while Maggie's father and another man awkwardly carried in the old copper caldron suspended on a pole.

"It goes right over there in the corner," Maggie's father said, straining with the oversized, sooty kettle. "Watch it doesn't rub against you, Tom," he said.

Once it was in place he said, "You about ready, Mag?"

"Just about, Daddy," she said.

"Need a ride, Tom?" he said.

"Yes I do, thank you," Tom said.

"Okay, I'll only be a couple more minutes," he said, closing the door behind him.

Maggie and Tom were alone again.

"Have you thought about what we were talking about before?" Tom said. "You know, about you and me? You know."

Maggie grinned from ear to ear. "Yep," she said. "I've been thinking about it. A lot."

"So what do you think?" Tom asked.

"It sounds better and better to me. It takes a little while to shake off the old lady and become the young girl with the hormones."

"So what do you think?" Tom said again.

"Hang in there, lad," Maggie said.

Tom smiled. "What does that mean?"

"It means," Maggie said, mock toasting him with a glass of soapy water and suds, "here's looking at you, Kid," she said in her best imitation of Humphrey Bogart.

Tom shrugged. "Okay," he said and took a swig of his birch beer. "Whatever that means."

Chapter Thirty-Five

Monday it rained.

Alfie ambled into Cragle's general store as Smokey Joe was coming out. He wandered past the locked postmaster's cage and shot a quick glance at the wicker basket and saw it was empty.

"Mr. Cragle," he said to the bespectacled, white haired man who ran the store, "if you'll sort of let me hang out here for a spell, I'll sweep your whole floor."

Cragle gave him a sideways glance and frowned. "What on earth would make you want to hang around for, Alfie? Haven't you got someplace you're supposed to be?"

"Well, it's raining," Alfie said, "and I've always had a hankerin' to run a general store when I grow up. And I thought I might pick up a few very important pointers from you."

Cragle nodded his head quickly in understanding. "Makes sense," he said. "Broom's back there. Don't raise too much dust."

Alfie's job was to make certain the envelope from Comstock and Comstock didn't show up on Monday for easy delivery on Tuesday to beat the Wednesday deadline. Had it not been raining, he would have sat outside and watched people coming in and out so he could spot the one with the envelope. But the rain drove him inside.

He saw nothing.

Meanwhile, Maggie and Tom sat in the drizzling rain huddled under a chestnut tree near Maggie's house where they could easily see the mailbox.

"What are you thinking about, Mag?" Tom asked.

"Oh, I don't know, Tom. About the stock market crash, I guess. Even if we don't go to New York, it's bound to hurt us. And then there's the depression. I already lived through that once."

"Well, it looks like you're going to get to do it again. This time in Cobblers Eddy — if we do things right."

"Yeah." She twisted the stem of a weed around her finger. "I wish there were a way I could warn people."

"Yeah."

"Course, nobody would believe me."

Tom didn't say anything.

"Would they, Tom? Nobody would believe me, would they?"

"A 16-year-old. No. Nobody would believe you. And it wouldn't matter if they did. You couldn't change things. You might be able to mess things up a bit. But you couldn't make them not happen. The stock market is still going to tumble. And there's still going to be a depression that will last for a decade."

"And if I warned people, what do you think would happen? I'd be right, you know. What I told them was going to happen would really happen. So what do you think?"

"You'd become a freak. And you wouldn't be able to change anything."

Maggie sighed. "A 16 year old freak oracle." She threw the twisted weed stalk to the ground. "But, damn it, Tom. I have a responsibility."

"A responsibility to who?"

"To whom," she corrected.

"A responsibility to whom?" he said.

"To everybody. To people. To those who are about to suffer."

"How do you know who's going to suffer?"

"Well, that's part of my problem. I don't know, for the most part. My dad will suffer. I know that."

"And you're doin' something about it. Otherwise, what are we doin' sittin' in the drizzling rain waitin' for Smokey Joe?"

"Yeah, but there must be a better way. This is so sneaky. Why can't I just tell my dad the truth?"

Tom laughed out loud.

"Tommm," she said. "Don't laugh at me. I don't like to be laughed at."

Tom shook his head from side to side trying to squelch his laughter. "I'm sorry, Maggie. I just can't help it. It brings up such funny pictures in my head. There's your dad and you about to have a serious talk. `Dad,' you say. `Sit down. I have something serious to tell you. First, Dad, I'm really a quarter of a century older than you are. Y' see, Dad, one afternoon about a week ago, I went to New York for 58 years. Are you still with me, Dad?'"

Maggie started to laugh a little in spite of herself, which encouraged Tom to unrestrained laughter. "I want to be there when you tell him about men walking on the moon and airplanes breaking the sound barrier. And color television sets. And `I Love Lucy' reruns."

"Tom, you rascal. You're baiting me, aren't you?"

"No, I'm serious," Tom doubled over with laughter. "So what if some screwball or another has been predicting the stock market would crash every day since God invented apples."

Maggie reached up and shook the rain water from a branch just above Tom's head. He laughed harder. "I want to be there when you tell your Dad about breath mints and the heartbreak of psoriasis." He rolled on the ground.

"Now stop it," Maggie said. She mussed his hair.

He looked at her seriously for a moment, fighting back a smile. Then suddenly he began to break up again. "Pac-Man," he said, as another laughing fit sputtered out of his mouth.

Maggie was on him, tickling him. "If you want to laugh, then let me help you," she said.

Tom rolled on the wet ground, laughing hysterically. He could hardly get his breath. "Digital watches. A Big Mac attack."

Maggie pulled out wet grass and threw it at him. She stuffed it down the front of his shirt. Tom got up to get away from her and Maggie tripped him back to the soggy ground. She leaped on him, clamped both hands on either side of his head and gave him a long, wet kiss full on the lips.

Tom's body relaxed. He looked at her for a moment, then

held her to him.

From the folds of his wet flannel shirt where she had buried her face, Maggie said at last, "That's the first passionate kiss I've had in more than 30 years."

Tom kept holding her. "I think it's the first I've ever had," he said.

When Smokey Joe showed up plodding along on his horse called "Horse," Maggie walked out to the gravel road to meet him. "Did we get any mail?" a soaking Maggie asked the rain drenched horseman.

"Yep. I think you got a thing or two. But I kin just put 'em in the mailbox for y'. I have to go by there anyway."

"No," Maggie said. "I'd like to have the mail now."

Smokey looked around at the soggy landscape. "Here?"

"Yes," Maggie said forcefully. "Here. And now."

Smokey shrugged and handed her a post card and an envelope, both addressed to her mother. He tipped his hat and rode on down the road.

Now she walked back to her house to deliver the mail and Tom trotted back down the hill toward the village to tell Gordie, who was waiting in the rain with his father's horse.

"No letter today, Gordie," he said. "Let's check with Alfie at the store, then go home."

On Tuesday, when Smokey Joe left to deliver his mail, Gordie was sitting in front of Cragle's store whittling a stick to a point. Periodically, he got up to see if anything was in the wicker basket — and to see that the county mail rider didn't come by with an out of town envelope. By the end of the afternoon, Gordie had a sore bottom from sitting on the ground so long, an impressive pile of wood shavings, and a very short stick.

Tom spent most of the afternoon waiting for word from Alfie that Smokey Joe had gone past Maggie's house without delivering the letter. They spent the rest of that sunny day stacking hay in the field just above Maggie's house.

The four conspirators considered Wednesday the most critical day. They took turns keeping an eye on the general store and the post office even in the morning while

Smokey Joe was working there. They did not know what Maggie's father may have said to Smokey Joe or whether the postman might make a special trip if the letter should arrive earlier then expected.

In the afternoon, Alfie, Gordie, and Tom took turns watching the general store.

About an hour after Smokey Joe left on his route, the county carrier came into the store and tipped his hat to Mr. Cragle. Whistling lowly to himself, he unlocked the post office cage, flipped a thick white envelope into the wicker basket, locked up again and left.

Tom glanced furtively at the envelope. He could see Maggie's father's name typed on the front and, in the upper left hand corner embossed in gold, he could see, Comstock and Comstock, New York. His heart jumped.

He got Alfie, who was waiting outside, to come in and sit by the post office cage. Mr. Cragle saw the boy waiting, looked knowingly at him over his glasses and handed him a broom. "You're going to make something of yourself, my lad," he said.

Tom ran at full speed to the junction of the gravel road, where Gordie was waiting with his father's horse.

He was so out of breath when he got there, he could hardly talk. "Tell Maggie. The letter. In the wicker basket. Hurry," he puffed.

The towering teenager climbed atop an even more massive horse and galloped up the hill.

When Gordie arrived with the news, Maggie was calm. "If the letter is down there now, and Smokey Joe is out delivering, I don't see the problem," she said.

Gordie looked puzzled. "Then why did Tom tell me to hurry?"

"Beats me," Maggie said with a shrug. "Here comes Smokes now."

Smokey Joe trotted slowly past Maggie and looked at her with suspicion. "Maggie, this is the third day in a row. An' you didn't get no mail." He glanced at Gordie and trotted on by.

They watched him go right on passed Maggie's house. Her father came out briefly, said something to Smokey. Smokey shook his head "no" and went on by.

"Yippee!" Maggie shouted. She grabbed Gordie by the elbows and started to dance with him.

"Watch, you'll scare my horse." Gordie said. Then he smiled a big toothy grin and threw his hat high in the air. "Yahahahoo! We did it, didn't we?"

"I think so," Maggie said. "We did it by not doing anything. Just keepin' our eyes open and our mouths shut."

"Hop on. I'll give you a ride down to Mrs. Moss's."

Maggie grabbed Gordie's belt and threw herself on the horse's back just behind the saddle. As they were riding, Gordie said, "You know, the first Wednesday the 30th, Mrs. Moss's pigs didn't get fed an' there was hell to pay."

At Mrs. Moss's, Maggie and Gordie filled the pigs' trough with sour milk, potato peels, sour bread, dried spoiled beans, meal, hay, corn, and green apples. The pigs seemed to love the sloppy mess and lowered their snouts deep into the full trough.

"Maggie." She heard a voice behind her. "It's here." She looked up and saw Smokey Joe on horseback waving a thick white letter in the air. "Your Daddy's letter from New York." He was galloping toward the gravel road. "He said he'd give me four bits if I could get it to him today. Yahoo!"

"No. Wait, Smokey, wait," Maggie cried.

"Not on your life. There's four bits awaitin' on this letter." He jabbed his heels into Horse and sailed on by.

Maggie ran up on Mrs. Moss's porch, almost running into the old lady, leaped onto the railing with one foot and flew through the air to the saddle of Gordie's colossal horse. She kicked her heels into the great, hulking beast and kept kicking until she was full gallop in pursuit of Smokey.

"Smokes, you better wait. I'm warnin' you," she called out breathlessly. "I need to talk to you."

"Sorry, Maggie, can't now. This is terrible important," Smokey Joe shouted over his shoulder. "As soon as I drop it off, we can talk all afternoon if you want."

Maggie's horse started to gain on him.

"Don't matter if you can catch up with me, Maggie," he yelled. "I ain't stoppin' for nobody. Hahaha! The mail is, by damned, goin' through. Move it, Horse." Smokey Joe took the horse up the gravel road like he was racing with the devil. "Yahoo!"

"Smokey. Stop. I've gotta have that letter." She pulled alongside him on her massive horse.

"Then ask yer pappy fer it," Smokey called out. "Cuz he's the one what's gettin' it. And not a moment too soon." He cut across the field of newly piled hay to get a more direct route to Maggie's house.

Maggie's horse was beginning to flag, and her house was just on the other side of the hedgerow. The horses were side by side when Maggie stood on top of the saddle and, leaping across, tackled Smokey Joe right into one of the haystacks.

They both disappeared into an explosion of hay which hid them for a moment then, like a trampoline, bounced them out again. As they emerged, spitting hay and flailing their arms, they could see letters falling through the air like snow flurries.

"Maggie, y' durn fool. Y' see what cha done? That's the U.S. mail, and you jest tampered with a whole bag full of it." He started picking up the mail. Maggie helped him.

"Here it is," he said holding the large white envelope in the air again.

Maggie grabbed it from him and ran towards Gordie's oversized mount. But the horse was spooked by all the excitement and moved away from her. She flipped herself on the back of Smokey's horse and rode off to the top of the hill again back toward the village and Mrs. Moss's.

"Wait, Maggie," Smokey was yelling at the top of his lungs. "Give me the letter." He had somehow gotten on top of Gordie's horse and was following her at a gallop. "That's the U.S. mail, Maggie. We're all goin' to be in a heap of trouble. Oh golly, Maggie. What's gotten into you?"

He was gaining on her, and she just kept going. Horse headed for Mrs. Moss's, and Maggie let him have his head. Gordie was still at Mrs. Moss's. And Maggie thought he'd be a handy one to have around if Smokey caught her.

She pulled up at Mrs. Moss's and dismounted just as Smokey was dismounting too. "Gimme that letter," Smokey said reaching for it. Maggie handed it to Gordie who was standing by the trough refilling it with slop. Gordie reached for it and missed. The letter dropped into the trough and disappeared.

Smokey quickly thrust his hand in the slop after it. Gordie pulled Smokey's hand back out. "Them pigs'll eat anything. Even your hand," he said.

Smokey pulled away and sat on the ground. He pushed back his hat and scratched his balding head. "I'll wait for them to empty the trough, then I'll get the letter. I may have lost my four bits, but the mail will go through."

As it happened, the mail must have gone through the pigs, because they cleaned the trough down to the wood and there was no letter to be seen.

"Oh, Lordie," Smokey said burying his head in his arms. "My career is a shambles. Maggie, your father will have my hide."

Maggie was smiling broadly. "Smokes. I've got a plan."

"Wull, tell me about it later. I got more mail to deliver now if my horse, Horse, ain't been ruined." He climbed into the saddle and slowly rode away.

Chapter Thirty-Six

As Smokey Joe delivered the remainder of his letters, he kept shaking his head, vowing never again to come within 10 feet of Maggie. He returned to the store to find the three boys and Maggie waiting for him with a package neatly wrapped and tied with a bow.

"Come on, Smokey, this is a peace offering." Maggie thrust the package at him.

There was nothing about the afternoon's events that amused Smokey. And, being tackled off his horse into a hay stack by a teenage girl was an indignity he would not soon forget. His face reddened. He pointed a finger at Maggie. "You tampered with the U.S. mail. That's no laughin' matter, Maggie."

"Ahh, come on, Smokey," Gordie said. "We didn't mean nothin'."

Smokey Joe pointed his finger toward Gordie. "An' you're the one that fed the envelope to them hogs. Yer in this thing up to yer neck, too. An' don't ferget it."

"Smokey, all we want to do is talk to you," Tom said. "Take the gift, Smokey. We want to be friends."

Smokey Joe looked at the package then turned up his nose and folded his arms, refusing to lift a hand to take it. "You open it," he said.

Maggie carefully peeled back the ribbon and paper to reveal four boxes of Red Man chewing tobacco.

Smokey refused to touch them. "Okay," he said, "What's in 'em."

"Tobacco."

"Yeah, an' what else?"

Alfie walked up to Maggie and took one of the boxes. He opened it and took out a pinch of tobacco, which he stuck in his mouth. He grimaced sourly and did not chew.

Maggie took a pinch too, as did Tom and Gordie.

"Here now," Smokey said. "You kids don't know how to chew tobakee proper. You're jest wastin' it." He accepted all the boxes. "Much obliged," he said, tipping his straw hat.

All four young people spit out their tobacco with obvious relief.

"We'll also make up the four bits to you, Smokey," Gordie said. "Jus' give us a little time."

"Nah," Smokey said. "That ain't necessary. The tobakee is plenty. But what was so consarned important about that envelope that you should carry on like that, Mag?"

"I can't tell you exactly, but I will tell you this: If my dad had gotten that envelope, my whole family would have left Cobblers Eddy and we'd have never been back."

"Yer whole family?"

"Yep."

"Hmm. If it had just been you."

Maggie giggled.

A sudden thought struck Smokey. "What am I gonna tell yer pa?"

"Don't tell him anything," Maggie said. "Today was the last day to record those papers at the courthouse. He doesn't need the envelope anymore. And if none of the five of us tells him, he'll never know what happened to it."

Smokey thought about it for a moment. "He'll just think it got lost in the mail."

"Yes."

"When actually, it got eaten in the trough." Smokey began to laugh, showing a mouth full of long, tobacco stained teeth. "You can be sure I ain't about to tell him — or nobody else. I like bein' a postman. An' I plan to keep on bein' one for a long spell."

Chapter Thirty-Seven

M rs. Moss was stone faced as she viewed Tom and Maggie from her kitchen window. "That young man touches her too much," she thought. "And the young girl acts as if she enjoys it. Land sakes!"

Maggie *did* enjoy it. She enjoyed virtually everything that had happened to her since her return from 1984. But preventing her father from going to New York was the icing on the cake. It had not gone smoothly, this attempt to manipulate time and events. The envelope seemed to have a life of its own, a will to get into the hands of her father. But in the end, they had pulled it off. The letter had disappeared safely into the stomachs of one or more of Mrs. Moss's grand old pigs.

When they finished talking with Smokey, Alfie went back into Guy Cragle's store to finish a job of sweeping he'd begun and to announce his retirement as Mr. Cragle's assistant in training. Gordie mounted his father's horse and slowly rode it home, leaving Tom and Maggie alone.

The young couple crossed the concrete road, then took a short cut over the hill. Tom spotted a Monarch butterfly flitting across the fields and tried to catch it in his cupped hands. But the butterfly evaded him.

"You'll never catch him in your hands," Maggie shouted after him, taking up the chase.

The butterfly landed on the edge of some dried cow manure in the field beyond the Goss's house.

Tom stopped. "Shhh," he said. "I'm going to come up on her blind side."

"Butterflies don't have blind sides," Maggie said.

"Shhh," Tom said. "She doesn't know she doesn't have a blind side." He took long, slow strides on his tiptoes.

Maggie crept as he crept, a few feet behind him, stepping in his footprints as he vacated them and imitating his gestures. "What are you going to do with him when you catch him?"

"Shhh, it's a her."

"How can you tell?" Maggie whispered.

"It doesn't have a penis."

Maggie giggled into her hand. "You must have incredible eyesight," she said.

The butterfly left its perch and dipped and dived across the field. "Whoa," Tom said as he and Maggie ran after it until it went high into the sky and crossed the hedgerow.

"What were you going to do with it if you caught it?" Maggie asked.

"What do you mean, *if* I caught it? You can't catch a butterfly with your bare hands. You need a net. You spent too many years in the city, girl," he mocked.

She kicked him playfully in the seat of the pants, and, as she did, he caught her foot and held her standing on one leg. "Look what I found," he said.

"Tom," she shrieked playfully. "Let go, I'm going to fall."

Tom began walking slowly still holding her leg so she had to hop along to keep up with him.

She put a hand on his shoulder to steady herself. "Tom, let go. Let go," she shouted.

Tom stopped walking, but held on to her foot. "Maybe we ought to talk about this," he said.

With her hand still on his shoulder, she said, "Let go of my foot, and then we'll talk about it."

"No, actually, I think I'd be more comfortable holding on to your foot. After all, you're the girl who kicked me in the seat of the pants, aren't you?"

"Absolutely not. That must have been someone else," she said.

Tom began walking some more to make her hop.

"Tom, Tom," she shouted. "Stop it, or else."

"Ho, ho, ho," Tom said. "Tough guy, eh? Or else, what?"

"Or else, this," she said as she crooked her elbow around

his neck and, pushing off with the only foot she had on the ground, leaped into his arms.

Tom fell backwards onto the ground and Maggie bounced off him, then onto her feet and into a run over the hill. Tom caught up with her and gave her a hug, lifting her off the ground and swinging her around. They both laughed, hugged again, and walked over the hill holding hands and swinging their coupled arms as they went.

"I'll see you tomorrow in the good morning," Tom said as he dropped Maggie off at her house and headed for his own.

"And every good morning thereafter," Maggie called back from her doorway.

She went inside and saw her father standing there by the window. He waved to Tom, then turned to her. "You seem happy," he said.

"Am I ever," she said. "I cannot tell you how happy." She gave him a hug, and when he began to relax his grip, she continued to hold him until he tightened his grip on her again. "Boy, I love you, Daddy," she said. "I'm such a lucky girl. I wish I could tell you how lucky."

He took his arms away from around her, then took her hands in his. "Sweetheart, you don't know how lucky you are. I have the most exciting news you can imagine."

"Oh-oh," she said casting a sideways glance at him. "What kind of good news?"

"It's a surprise. One peach of a surprise."

"I don't think I like surprises," she said. "What kind of a surprise is it?"

"I want to wait until your mother is here. Then I'll tell you."

"Please tell me now, Daddy. I want to know."

"Ahh," he said, mulling it over. "Sure. Why not? I'll tell you now, Sweetheart. In two weeks, we'll all be living in New York City." He smiled broadly, waiting for her response.

She began to cry. He held her close to him again.

"There, there, Sweetheart. I know it's sudden. I didn't want to get your hopes up."

She pulled away. "How can that be? The letter didn't come by the deadline," she said.

"How did you know about the letter?" he asked. "Did your mother tell you?" He thought about it for a moment. "I'm surprised. Anyway, when the letter didn't arrive, I went down to Guy Cragle's and made a long distance phone call to New York. They were surprised the letter hadn't arrived on time, but they were willing to bend the rules a little — just for us. So we're going anyway — letter or no letter." He squeezed her again. "So how do you like them apples, Maggie?" he said.

It was Margaret Stone who leveled Maggie's eyes at this incredibly naive man who had once long ago been her father but was now her junior by nearly 30 years.

"Daddy," she said, after a long moment of silence, "we've got to have a talk."

"Sure, Sweetheart, I'll tell you all about it."

"Not about New York. I have something I've got to tell you." She couldn't believe her own words. Was she really going to tell him about New York and why she didn't want to go? Was she really going to tell him the all time most unbelievable fantasy?

She was. She knew she was. She had to. Her love for her father required it.

"How about now," her father's voice was saying.

"Now?" She said.

"No time like the present."

She sat down. "Definitely not now," she said.

"What's the matter with now? Huh?" Her father's playfulness was returning. He bent over her chair and gave her a kiss on the top of her head. "Do we need to set up an appointment?"

"It's going to take some time."

"How much?"

"Three hours."

"You're kidding."

"No, I'm not."

"Three hours? Why so long?"

"I need that much time to tell my story."

"But three hours, Maggie. What are you going to tell me that takes three hours?

"I'm going to tell you." she said, pausing. "How I know," she stopped mid-sentence, "you're planning to go to New

York City."

"Can't you just say, Joe Blow told you — or whoever?"

"No."

"But three hours, Maggie. Be reasonable."

"Three uninterrupted hours."

"Why you little squirt. Are you telling me I can't talk?"

"Yes."

"I have to sit there and listen? To you?"

"Yes."

"For three hours?"

"Yes."

"Why you little squirt."

"There are some other rules, too."

"Good Lord, Maggie. What?" He tried to make light of Maggie's demands, but he was clearly disquieted.

"You can't make any judgments."

He folded his arms. "What else?"

"We have to be alone, undisturbed. You can't ask me to stop. You can't be insulted. Or angry." She looked at him.

He stared at her for a time without saying anything. "When I was a boy," he said at last, "there was an apple tree at the edge of the orchard. When I wanted to be alone, I used to crawl up under its branches and stare down across the fields to the woods." He watched her for a long moment. "No one will disturb us there," he said.

"Okay."

"Sunday, after dinner. Just you and me."

"Okay, Daddy." She stood up.

"This better be good."

"I don't think you're going to like it."

"Then don't tell me."

"I have to."

He stared at her in silence again. Then he winked at her. "Then do it," he said.

Chapter Thirty-Eight

"I feel like I'm going on a date," Maggie's father said as he walked with his arm slung across her shoulders, her arm wrapped around his waist. They walked slowly.

"Your mother and I used to go up here to the orchard. I asked her to marry me there as we looked out over the fields and the lowlands. We came back here again and again. No one knew where we were. It's so quiet, and you can see for miles and miles." He looked at Maggie and smiled. "I thought it was a big deal — showing her the place that had been exclusively and privately mine since I was a child. And now," he said, "I'm going up to the same old place with my sweet daughter, Maggie."

Maggie smiled and squeezed him, but didn't say anything.

They walked the rest of the way in silence. There was a break in the stone wall that separated the orchard from the dirt road. "Look out for poison ivy," her father said as he stood aside so she could pass through first. They walked through tall grass between trees with graceful branches arched with heavy green apples.

"I should prop those limbs up before we leave or they'll break off," he said. He shook his head. "I've got to stop fretting about the farm. Soon it won't be my worry."

They walked down a gradual incline to a rocky area that led to a more abrupt drop to the lower part of the orchard and beyond. "I keep the brush cut down there so it won't block the view. But this is the first time I've sat down to enjoy the view in years." He sat on the ground and leaned back on the incline, looking out over the fields below. "This is the life," he said.

Maggie said nothing, but stood slightly behind him winding a timothy stem around her finger.

He looked back at her suddenly. "Well, go ahead. You've got three hours," he said.

Maggie exhaled heavily. "Boy," she said finally, "I don't know where to begin."

"Begin at the beginning."

"But it's all about time. And this is the beginning. I want to tell you about the end and how dreadful it was," she said.

"Are you going to tell me about the change in you? Why you sound different? Why you use different words? Like `dreadful?'"

She didn't answer.

"Well are you?"

"Oh, yes. I am. I'm sorry. I was thinking." She sat cross legged on the ground opposite him. She looked him straight in the eye, and when his gaze was locked on hers for a moment, she began:

"I am telling you this because I love you. And because I don't want you to go to New York. And because I don't want to keep my biggest secret from you for the rest of my life. I have not told anyone else and probably never shall. Tom and Alfie and Gordie know because they are a part of it."

"You still haven't told me anything."

"It's supernatural, Daddy. It couldn't happen. But it did."

Her father sat up. A look of concern crossed his face. "What happened, Maggie?"

She shook her head. "No, it's not that simple. I can't just tell you what happened. It's too incredible." She looked at him again. "And don't be too understanding. When I get done telling you, you're going to be angry or hurt or worried about me or.."

"For the love of Pete, Maggie, will you tell me about it?"

"Okay. Let me tell you a story. No, let me tell you what happened just a few days ago. Tom and Alfie and Gordie and I went on a picnic down by Jim Kocher's field. The train came by, real slow, and we hopped on, danced around a bit, then hopped off. Then Alfie started acting weird; said we had made a second jump, but not yet."

"Deja vu?"

"No. Deja vu is when you think it has happened before. This was a premonition. Alfie said this was *going* to happen." She sighed heavily again. "I think I'm hyperventilating," she said with a self conscious smile. "This has all been so long ago, I'm not sure what exactly happened next. Somehow, I heard you telling Mom that you were going to New York if a certain envelope came in the mail on time."

"But I thought . . . "

Maggie held up her hand. "Now wait, let me finish. Anyway, somehow I ended up on Smokey Joe's horse and got the letter to you just in time, and you and I drove like blazes to the courthouse, and we made it on time. And then you and Mom and I moved to New York."

"That was quite a dream."

"No, wait a minute, Daddy. Let me tell it. It was not a dream. It happened. We went to New York. We lived in a big old brownstone at 409 East 72nd Street and you worked for Comstock and Comstock on Wall Street. I finished up high school at the Barstow School, then went on to NYU and you got very, very rich. Mom hated New York. J.J. Reardon killed himself. The stock market crashed and the depression hit. You went broke. And those sweet boys were lost forever in a boxcar when they tried to come up to see me. And it was so terribly awful." She looked down shaking her head and began to sob.

Her father put his arm around her and she leaned against him and cried loudly, her face wet with tears. He just held her and said, "Take your time, Maggie. Take your time. I'll listen. Don't get upset. We've got lots of time."

When she regained her composure, she began telling him the whole story in greater detail. They both evaded the other's eyes, looking instead out into the farmlands below. Maggie's voice was mechanical and unemotional as she described the joys and tragedies of her life in New York. Her father was silent for a long time, then began asking questions now and again. His voice did not betray any emotion either. Maggie could not tell from his demeanor what he believed and what he did not. He seemed like someone receiving bad news and trying to buck up under it as best he could.

Maggie told him everything, sparing him nothing. As they spoke, there were long pauses between statement and reaction, question and answer.

"I remember when you died," Maggie said.

Long silence.

Her father sighed heavily. "I don't think I want to know."

"It doesn't matter if you know. It won't happen just that way again. It can't. Too much has happened to alter it."

He glanced at her quickly, then turned away again. "I could die sooner," he said.

"Yes, but not likely."

"Your mother?"

"She lived to be very old. Ninety-four."

"She was alone." He looked at Maggie for verification. "Was she alone? Did she remarry?"

"No. She was alone."

"That's terrible. I don't know which is worse. I don't want her to be alone."

After a long pause, Maggie said softly, "Does that mean you're not going to go?"

"No, that's not what it means. It may change a lot of things. But I'm still going to New York."

Maggie's tone changed now. She was exasperated and showed it. "You don't believe a word I've told you, do you? You think I made up this fantastic story to get you to stay here so I could be with my friends, don't you?"

"No, Maggie, of course not."

"Then why on earth would you go? If you believed one word of what I've said . . . " she began to sputter, "you don't . . . you won't. I mean, how could you still want."

"You don't seem to understand, Maggie. I am going to New York. I have to go. Even if all you say is correct. Even if I fail and die in the attempt. Even if it all turns out to be the worst kind of a nightmare. I. Am. Going. My life is in New York. In the stock market. On Wall Street. I haven't lived yet. And I'm going to. Nobody can cheat me out of that. What happens if I stay on the farm? Do you know? Did you live through that one too?"

He took her hand in his. "I'm sorry, Maggie. I don't mean

to be making light of what you've just told me. But whether you're 16 or 60 million years old, you still can't understand the imperative of my life. I was not put here to sell insurance and prop up the overburdened branches of those apple trees. Or to cut the brush. Or milk cows at 6 o'clock in the morning. I have a brain, and energy, and imagination. In whatever time I've got in this life, I want to take the world by the scruff of the neck and shake the hell out of it."

"But that's not the way it will happen. You did everything right. You built a fortune in no time.

"No I didn't, Maggie. That's just the point. I haven't built any fortune. I built a chicken coop, and that's as far as it's ever going to go if I don't get out of here."

"But, Daddy, it didn't work. It was an unreal world. What's going on in New York at this very moment is insanity. The banks are chasing their own money. They're loaning money to people to buy stocks. It's the banks' money that's chasing up the value of stocks. It's just one big game of `Let's Pretend.' Everyone is pretending. It can't go on. And toward the end of 1929, it stops. The whole thing falls down. People lose their savings. Banks go belly up. Industries fold. This country goes into the greatest economic depression the world has ever known." She got to her feet and raised her voice. "And I'm not dreaming. I was there," she trumpeted.

Her father got to his feet, somewhat less agilely than Maggie had. He dusted off the seat of his pants. "Come here, Maggie," he said calmly. "Give me a hug."

She came over and gave him a hug. "I'm sorry, Daddy. It's just that . . ."

He continued to hold on to her. "It scares me, Maggie, when you shout. Have I ever heard you shout before?"

She held on to him. "I'm sorry," she said again. "You are so precious to me. Have I changed your mind about anything? Has this past three hours done anything other than make you think your daughter is a bit crazy?"

He released her and looked at his watch. "I don't think you're crazy. I think you believe what you said is true. But, no, I don't think you went forward in time."

They began walking back toward the house.

"Darn it," Maggie said. "I didn't tell it right." She looked at him again. "If I had told it right, you'd have believed it."

He shook his head. "Maggie, it has nothing to do with how you told it. I can't believe it."

"Oh," Maggie said.

"Come on, Mag. It's not that I don't believe anything that can't be proven. It's just . . . I don't know, that's in a special category. I know there's a lot we don't understand: how some people like Alfie can see the future, how thoughts can get from one person's mind into another's, wild coincidences that are too far fetched to really be coincidences. People with strange abilities. Even people who die and then come alive again. I don't understand that stuff, but I keep an open mind. Y' know what I mean? It doesn't threaten me. I don't have a great investment in believing otherwise. So maybe there are ghosts somewhere. Or maybe an evil spirit here and there. It doesn't really warm the cockles of my heart, but I don't care a lot either." He reached down and picked up a stone and threw it back toward the orchard.

"Daddy, you're such a kid."

"Perhaps not as much as you think. There are things I'm inflexible about; things I do care about. They are a part of the structure of my life. They never change, not for me and not for anybody else. There are always 24 hours in a day. There is always a morning and an evening in every day. It gets dark at night. We need air and food to survive. Those kinds of things are cornerstones of life. There's always a summer and a fall, winter and spring. History is always in the past and the future hasn't happened yet. One always comes before two and three always comes after two."

He held her at arms length and looked deep into her eyes. "Maggie, my father was always older than me, and my daughter is always going to be younger. Always, Maggie. It will never change. Not ever. If by some further magic I had been with you and experienced those future years in New York and then returned to finish out the day, I still wouldn't believe it."

"Then how do you explain all I've told you? How could I know all I know?"

"I don't have to explain it. There's a whole lot of stuff I

don't understand in this world. What you've just told me simply joins the list."

"You do believe what I've told you about New York and the stock market, don't you?"

"Yes."

"Why?"

"I don't know. I think you can see it. I can accept that you can see it."

They walked down the gravel road toward the house. "Are you still going to New York?" Maggie asked.

"Yes."

Maggie stopped walking. After a few steps, her father stopped too. He looked back at her. Maggie didn't look at him. "I'll miss you," she said.

Her father approached her and gazed intently into her eyes as if he were seeing something deep within. He understood. "I'll miss you too," he said as he continued to stare. Then he added a message of his own. "And I'll miss your mother."

Chapter Thirty-Nine

Maggie found Tom late in the afternoon finishing up the milking alone. "Your dad's not here?" she asked.

"Nah, he's getting ready for the fireworks tonight." Tom shook his head.

"Why are you shaking your head?" she asked.

"Cuz there aren't going to be any fireworks tonight," he said.

"Yes there are. My dad's got it all set. That's what I wanted to tell you. He decided to go to New York tomorrow, now that Mom and I aren't going. And he's not mortgaging the farm. He might have left today if he didn't have to set off the fireworks tonight."

"He really takes that job of setting off the firecrackers serious, doesn't he?" Tom said.

"Serious enough. Next year they'll have to get somebody else to do it. Tonight's his last."

"Maggie, there won't be any fireworks tonight. Don't you remember?"

Maggie was puzzled. "Remember what? What's going to happen, Tom?" she said.

"Oh, Maggie, I thought you remembered. But of course you wouldn't after all this time. Today is Mrs. Moss's last day."

"Last day for what?"

"Her last day. She will die tonight."

"What?" she shouted. "She's going to die?"

"Oh, Maggie," Tom came over to Maggie and put an arm around her shoulders. "Maggie, I'm so sorry. I didn't mean to tell you like that. She'll die tonight, just before the fireworks start."

Maggie pulled away. "Then there's still time. We've got to do something."

"What can we do? She's an old, old lady with an old heart that just stops. What can we do?"

"Oh!" Maggie shouted in anger and disgust. She spun on her heel. "This is so awful." She looked Tom in the eye again. "You poor sweetheart," she said, "Knowing what's going to happen must be a terrible strain." She put her arms around him and held on to him for a few minutes. "What does she die of?" Maggie asked.

"She dies of being old," Tom said. "She's sitting there, all dressed up in a fancy dress watching folks go by on their way to the fireworks. The next thing, she's slumped over. They take her inside, but she's already gone."

"So they canceled the fireworks?"

"Of course, it'd be an insult to have the fireworks right after she died. Don't you think so?"

"Yes," Maggie said. "I do. I most certainly do." She smiled rather pleasantly. The worry lines left her brow. She seemed transformed, as if thinking of some time and place far away. She looked into Tom's face. "This is such a lovely place, Tom. People are important here, aren't they?"

"Wouldn't they have done the same thing in New York? In 1984?"

"I don't know. I hope they would." A far away look came into her eyes as she continued to hold on to Tom. "When President Kennedy was shot in 1963, they had some kind of a big football game scheduled that day or the next, and they played the game anyway. A lot of people were incensed about it."

July Fourth was a hot, breezeless Sunday in 1926. Mrs. Moss went to church in the morning, then fixed herself a bowl of vegetable soup and a cup of sassafras tea for lunch. She hoed her vegetable garden in the afternoon until the heat drove her back indoors. In the hottest part of the afternoon, she went upstairs, opened a trunk and took out a wrinkled, black dress with lace at the neck and sleeves. She hung the dress in the open air on the front porch for a time while she sat in her rocking chair and fanned herself.

Later she took the dress inside and ironed it. Mrs. Moss thought it frivolous to change one's clothes in the middle of the day. But it was Sunday, and a holiday and her birthday. So, she changed anyway. To be sure no one saw, she pulled the blinds and locked the doors while she put on the dress. She looked in the mirror and scowled at her own image, then went back to her rocking chair on the front porch to escape the heat once more. She rocked for a time, then just as it was getting dark and people were collecting for the fireworks display, closed her eyes, slumped in her chair, and stopped rocking forever.

Chapter Forty

The Rev. J. Alends Jones moved slowly to the pulpit, spread a book before himself, folded his hands and cast a beatific smile over most of the residents of Cobblers Eddy and the surrounding farms.

"It appears," he said in round, preachery tones, "that Sunday morning has arrived on Tuesday afternoon, this week." He smiled down on those before him. "I am deeply gratified to see such a gathering before me as we celebrate the long, exemplary life, recently suspended, of the oldest member of our community, Mrs. Selina Anne Pierce Moss, wife of the late Alfred C. Moss and daughter of pioneer Arlote Quincy Pierce, one of the first settlers of this part of the country.

"Mrs. Moss, as she has been affectionately known for most of our lives, I dare say all of our lives, was 100 years old on the day she died."

There was a hum through the assemblage. The Rev. Mr. Jones waited.

"There is more," he said, thrusting an extended index finger into the air. "This dear lady, whose earthly remains lie before you, was more, much more than you may have thought. She was born on July 4, 1826, on the 50th anniversary of the signing of the Declaration of Independence, that greatly revered document which formed the cornerstone of this great country of ours." He leaned over the pulpit and added in softer, somewhat confidential tones: "She was born on the very day, July 4, 1826, on which two of the greatest presidents and patriots this nation has ever known departed this earth. Yes, my friends, this humble woman was born on the day both President Thomas Jefferson and President John Adams, ahh, expired."

He pressed the palms of his hands together before him. "My friends, this dear woman of our community is your window to the past. And, Lord God willing, your inspiration for the future." He pointed to the coffin. "She lies there as mute testimony to the continuity of things past and things which are yet to be. So let her be an inspiration to those of us who are left behind to toil in God's great vineyards, an inspiration to dedicate ourselves to the Christian ideals demonstrated in the exemplary life of Selina Anne Pierce Moss. Let us pray."

In the moment of silence that followed, Maggie's father whispered to her: "What do you think of our preacher?"

She whispered back, "He's an ass."

A quick laugh sputtered from her father's lips before he got himself more or less under control. For the remainder of the service he fought off the worst case of the giggles he'd had since he was a teenager himself.

While Maggie's mother helped prepare food in the church kitchen following the service, Maggie and her father joined the others walking slowly behind the coffin as it was carried up the concrete road beyond Mary Cragle's house to a small, carefully manicured plot at the top of the hill.

"Life is deceptive, isn't it, Mag," Maggie's father said as they walked. "Maybe unpredictable is a better word." He continued to trudge along, not seeming to need an answer to his questions. "Mrs. Moss probably did as well as any of us will. She lived a long time. She took care of herself. Didn't bother a whole lot of folks. Enjoyed her life. I guess she did. I don't know for sure. Then she died without any fuss. That's quite a trick."

He walked on in silence for a few moments, then continued. "I can understand one person's mind influencing another," he said. "I might even be able to accept the notion that a boy with Alfie's special gifts could unknowingly plant his own flights of fancy into the minds of his closest friends . . . and make them seem real."

Maggie knew there was more to come.

"I've had a chance to do some thinking, Mag," he said at last. "When Alfie, Gordie and Tom jumped off the train, you said they had bags of clothes with them, right?

"That's right," Maggie said. She suddenly understood her father's logic. "That would be the proof, wouldn't it? There must have been something among their clothes that we bought in 1984. There's got to be."

"It'd only take one thing from 1984 to make me a believer," her father said.

"I'll ask them. They must have gone back by now to get their stuff.

"Back where?"

"Back to Jim Kocher's field," Maggie said. "They didn't bring the clothes along when we went to Mrs. Moss's. So they must have gone back to get them."

"Or else they're still there."

"Right."

"Or maybe they're not still there," Maggie's father said.

"You don't think they'll be there?"

"I don't know. Did they have money in their pockets — 1984 money? A pocket knife? A pack of chewing gum? Anything?

"Not money. I had the money. They probably didn't have anything. Maybe some wadded up old Kleenex in their pockets.

Her father looked at her. "Kleenex?" he said.

"Ahh, they're soft paper hankies."

Her father looked at her blankly.

"It doesn't matter. They'd be long gone by now even if they did prove anything."

"How about the clothes they were wearing?"

"I think they were wearing the same clothes they arrived in — or nearly so." She looked at her father. "They'd been laundered a few times."

"By a laundry?"

"No. By automatic washing machine."

"By automatic?"

"Yes, they were washed in my automatic washing machine. Several times."

"Automatic washing machine? Too bad you couldn't have brought one of those back."

They walked in silence for a few moments.

"I wonder if you're right — about bringing back anything, I mean." Maggie said.

"That's a possibility you really ought to consider. We can ask the boys if they've got anything from 1984. But I'm not very hopeful. Surely you'd have heard about it by now. Or seen it."

"You think?" Maggie asked.

They followed Mrs. Moss's funeral procession as it turned off the main road and crossed the corner of Mary Cragle's orchard on their way up the hill to the cemetery.

"Let me ask you something else, Maggie," her father said. "How many histories do you think there are?"

"Meaning what?"

"Meaning, there's only one. There may be several versions in history books. But there's only one history as it really happened. And it's behind us. It started with the dawn of time and it includes everything that has happened every place in the universe from the dawn of time until this precise instant."

"Okay."

"At some point, the future — that time between now and 1984 — will be history, right?"

"Yes."

"There will only be one history of that period too, won't there?"

"Yes there will." Maggie said with some energy. "And I know what it will be because I was there."

Her father shook his finger. "No. You don't know what it will be like. Maybe you were there and maybe you weren't. I don't know. What I do know is that what you saw and experienced isn't going to happen the way you saw it and experienced it."

"Yes, but . . . "

"Do you remember the first day your mother and you and I arrived in New York?"

"Like it was tomorrow."

"Well, that experience is never going to happen. It exists nowhere in the world — no where in the whole universe —

except in your head. And it never will exist anywhere except in your head."

"If you're trying to confuse me, you're doing a very good job," Maggie said.

"I'm trying to get you to see this phenomenon for what it really is. It's little Alfie who has planted the idea in your head. Alfie is just a little boy. And this special gift he has is more than he can control. God only knows how, but somehow he brought you and Alfie and Tom into his dream world.

"You mean . . . you think . . . are you saying I'm still 16, not 16 again?"

Her father nodded. "Exactly. You're still Maggie. Not Maggie again. That's the only explanation. And I want you to accept it and get on with the fun of being 16 and sweet as a slice of apple pie."

Maggie thought about it for a moment. "But everyone says I'm different than I was."

"But, you see . . . "

"Yeah, I know. That would come with Alfie's dreamin'." She walked on for a few moments with a smile on her face, which her father noticed.

"I've seen that look before, Maggie. What scheme are you hatching?"

"I like your premise," she said. "I'm not sure I believe it, but I'm going to accept it anyway."

"Terrific," her father said. "That's just wonderful. What's the catch?"

"Two conditions. I'll accept your premise if you'll do two things for me."

"Oh oh, this sounds like trouble."

"No, I'm serious. You have to promise."

"Before I've heard what they are?"

"Yes."

He signed heavily. "I wonder if other fathers do these foolish things. Okay, I promise."

"First, I want you to take all the money you can shake loose and buy IBM stock."

"IBM stock? What do you know about IBM stock?"

"That's the first thing. The second thing is I want you to sell every bit of stock you've bought on margin."

"What do you know about buying on margin?"

Maggie pressed on. "Will you do it?"

He didn't answer right away. He stared at the ground, then spoke in somber tones. "My plan was to go to New York and get rich." He looked at her now. "That has been the plan for longer than I can remember. I didn't want to work on Wall Street just because I studied investment finance. I studied investment finance because I wanted to work on Wall Street."

He said no more, but walked in silence to the top of the hill. There in the bright sunshine was a blue and white striped canvas canopy. Folding wooden chairs were lined up inside and spilled slightly beyond its confines. The earth from the open grave at the far end of the canopy was covered by canvas. As the casket was laid on heavy canvas straps across the opening, the Rev. Mr. Jones read the 23rd Psalm. Then the assemblage broke up into small groups, each choosing its own path and pace back to the village of Cobblers Eddy. There, as was the custom, a reception was held at the church.

"That's how it was planted in my mind." Maggie's father continued as if he had never stopped. "My greatest dream was my career. I knew it would come some day. I was hardly even surprised when the Comstocks made me an offer." He continued to walk at a more brisk pace.

"But do you know what, Maggie? While I was dreaming that dream, I was living a bigger one. You. You and your mother." He smiled at her and seemed very much in the present, not vague and distracted as he had on the way up. "Now I have to make a choice between dreams. And suddenly, there is no choice." He stopped and, facing Maggie, took both her hands in his. "Maggie," he said, "you know what? I betcha I'm not going to New York."

Maggie was dumbfounded. She swallowed hard. A thin voice she hardly recognized as her own said, "You're not?" She cleared her throat and said it again in a lower register. "You're not? That's wonderful. But why?"

Her father took out a cloth handkerchief and wiped the perspiration from his neck, then replaced the handkerchief in his back pocket.

"I don't know exactly. Too much of what's important is

here. In Cobblers Eddy." He didn't look at her, but walked along as if trying to make sense of his own words. "I don't know," he said again.

Maggie walked silently with him, a long, broad smile playing across her lips. She remained silent as long as she could. Finally a long, low "Yahoo!" whooped from her throat. She jumped on her father and threw her arms around his neck, almost knocking him off balance. She kissed him a dozen times in rapid succession.

He blushed. "Maggie. There are people watching." He looked around. "Anyway, nobody should be that happy at a funeral." They both started to laugh. He grabbed her hand and gave it a squeeze.

When they got back to the church, they went into the kitchen and found Maggie's mother.

"Daddy has something to tell you," Maggie said pulling her father by the hand.

"I'm not going to New York, and I'm not going to be rich," he said.

"He *is* going to be rich, Mom," Maggie said with a wink.

"Oh, John," his wife said as she dried her hands on a dish cloth. Ignoring the other women in the kitchen, she walked up to him and put her arms around him and held him with her eyes closed for a moment. "I'm so happy," she whispered in his ear.

"Hey Maggie." Tom poked his head in the door from the Sunday school room where food was being laid out for those who stopped by. "Maggie, who is Calvin Klein?"

Maggie walked quickly across the kitchen and into the Sunday School room, closing the door behind her. Gordie and Alfie joined Tom and her from across the room.

"Who is Calvin Klein?" Gordie asked brightly.

"Shhh." Maggie said. "Come here, Gordie." She got all three in a huddle at the far end of the room. "Don't call out stuff like that."

"Why not?"

"People will hear you. Hey, Daddy's not going to New York. He just decided."

All three boys faces lit up.

"How'd ya get him to stay? That's wonderful," Tom said.

"I didn't do anything. He just decided not to go because

he'd miss us — Mom and me — because we weren't going."

"Well don't that beat all?" Gordie said. "After all our work, he just up and decides to stay on his own?" He shook Maggie's hand a little awkwardly.

Maggie frowned. "What's this about Calvin Klein?"

"He's got his name on my overalls and my mom wanted to know who he is," Gordie said.

"What'd you tell her?"

Gordie shrugged. "I told her the truth. I don't know who he is."

"Didn't she want to know where you got the pants from . . . wait a minute. Those are the pants I bought for you in New York, so you would have pants that fit when we went to the Palm Court. You must have brought them back from 1984. You surely brought them back from 1984. Aha! My proof."

"I told her you and Tom got `em for me."

Maggie was smiling. "My proof." She looked around the room and saw her father sit in a chair and begin eating potato salad from a plate balanced on his knee. She headed for him. "Maggie," Gordie protested. "Where you goin'?"

"I'm going to tell my Dad."

"That I got Calvin Klein's pants?"

"You bet."

"What good will that do?" Tom asked.

Maggie stopped. "I'll tell you what good it will do. It'll prove to him that I'm twice as old as he is and four times as old as I look and I am not crazy."

"You mean he knows Calvin Klein?" Gordie said.

"No, Gordie," Tom said. "How would he know Calvin Klein?" Alfie shook his head in agreement.

"Right," Maggie said.

"Oh," Gordie said, and turned to walk away. He stopped and turned around again. "I don't get it. If he don't know who Calvin Klein is, then why . . . ?"

But Maggie was already gone. Tom watched her walk toward her father, hesitate, then approach him. Her father looked up. Maggie asked a question. Her father nodded affirmatively, then nodded toward the kitchen. Maggie turned and walked back to the boys.

"Gordie, there's some great — I mean *swell* — potato

salad out in the kitchen," she said.

"I don't have to be told twice," Gordie said. He marched off toward the kitchen, followed by Alfie.

Maggie caught Tom's arm. "Let's go for a little walk, Tom," she said. She led him out the side door and along the path.

"Had your father heard of Calvin Klein?" Tom asked.

"Of course not. Calvin Klein probably hasn't been born yet."

"Well, what did he say?"

Maggie laughed a short, girlish giggle. "I asked him . . . " she laughed again. "I asked him if there was any more potato salad. And he said `yes, out in the kitchen.'"

"Maggie." There was a hint of exasperation in Tom's voice. "What was all that fuss you made about Gordie's Calvin Klein pants? You said you were going to tell your dad about the pants — 'proof, for once and for all,' you said."

Maggie stared at Tom for a moment, then averted her eyes. She shrugged. "Yeah," she said. "I did say that, didn't I?" She smiled. "Fortunately, I caught myself in the nick of time. I almost `snatched defeat from the jaws of victory,' as they say in the 80s."

"I still don't get it."

"There is nothing to be gained by convincing my father of anything. He's content that Alfie planted a fantasy in our minds. I got to tell him the whole truth and he figured out a way he and I could live with it. I don't have this big secret that I'm keeping from him. I don't have to go through my life with this incredible experience that I can't tell my dad. He knows. And he's explained it away. That's better than I ever dreamed of."

"You're not going to New York. That's what I dreamed of."

"We won it all, Tom. Daddy's not going to New York. We're not mortgaging the farm. And I get to be a kid again — and lead an entirely different kind of life."

Tom unconsciously folded her hand in his. "Yeah," he said. "I suppose that's right. But the pants are such a swell way to prove we were there."

"I'm not so sure my dad'd accept that as proof," Maggie said. "More likely if I told him, he'd argue with me about it.

And the battle would go on. And on and on."

Tom pulled up two timothy stalks. He stuck one in his mouth and stuck the other in Maggie's. He shrugged. "I suppose you know what you're doing. But you can't change your mind. It's really now or never. After Gordie's been wearing the overalls for a spell . . ."

"There're jeans."

"Yeah, whatever they are. After he's been wearing them a spell, it's going to be hard to convince your pa."

"Oh pooh," Maggie said. "The pants are a weak argument even now. Anyway, I brought back something else that no one could argue with. Proof positive if I ever wanted to use it."

"Wait a minute," Tom said. "You couldn't have brought anything back. You were an old lady in a flowery dress when you left the train and young Maggie when you landed in the grass. There was no way you could have brought back anything. Where would you carry it?"

"In my head," she said.

"Oh yeah. A lot of good that'll do."

"*What?*"

"You just spent two or three hours telling your father everything you could think of to convince him," Tom said. "And he didn't budge. Now, big news, there's something you can tell him that will turn him around immediately. That's an awful hard pill for me to swallow, Maggie."

"I didn't say it would turn him around. I just said it was irrefutable proof. And it's not something I would tell him. It's something I would demonstrate for him."

"Like what?" Tom asked as they walked.

Maggie leaned into him playfully. "This 16-year-old, country girl was educated in that one-room school house down the hill," she said playfully.

"So what?" Tom said leaning back toward her.

"So I speak French," she said. "Rather well, too, if I do say so myself." She paused to give Tom a chance to think about it. "They don't teach French in Cobblers Eddy or anywhere else around here." She smiled slyly. "That'd be kinda hard for my old dad to explain away." She swung her hips into Tom, knocking him off balance. *"N'est ce pas, mon cheri?"*

Before Tom could retaliate, Maggie turned and ran back toward the church. Laughing, Tom ran beside her, bumping her as he did and dodging her attempts to bump him back.

The end

About the author

Like the title character of this book, author JOHN D. HUSBAND spent his youth on his grandfather's farm and, as an adult, lived for a time in an old brownstone house in New York City. He has been a counter intelligence agent, newspaper reporter, advertising agency creative staffer, Washington news bureau chief, and an entrepreneur. The father of four grown children, he resides in suburban Washington DC.